Slaying for Sloan

WRECKED BOOK **THREE**

MELISSA MCSHERRY
DANA LEEANN

Slaying for Sloan

Wrecked Book **Three**

Melissa McSherry
Dana LeeAnn

TRIGGER WARNINGS

YOUR MENTAL HEALTH MATTERS.
READ THIS PAGE IN ITS ENTIRETY.

This book contains(but not limited to) content depicting explicit language, explicit sexual content, assault, murder, gaslighting, drowning, manipulation, brief mention of a pregnancy announcement (not the female main character), taboo religious content, blasphemy, reflection of child abuse (physical and mental), mention of rape, mutilation of a body, and knife play.

This book is not intended for readers under the age of 18. Read with caution. Your mental health matters.

The book you are about to read is DARK and not recommended for all readers. Read through the trigger warnings once more, then decide if you should continue on with this book. The content within this book is heavy.

PLAYLIST

A Nonsense Christmas - Sabrina Carpenter

Santa, Can't You Hear Me - Live - Nova Miller

One I've Been Missing - Little Mix

Baby I'm Coming Home - Ally Brooke

Snowman - Sia

Last Christmas - Ariana Grande

Christmas Tree Farm - Taylor Swift

Santa's Coming for Us - Sia

Winter Things - Ariana Grande

For those who want to be chased through the snow in a Hallmark village, and then fucked amongst the twinkling lights of the Christmas tree farm when he catches you

Chapter One
Sloan

Holly Grove.

The most magical place I've ever experienced during the holidays. It's most easily comparable to a Hallmark village. Twinkling lights, soft snowflakes blanketing the ground in a soft, leisurely descent, and a cool peppermint hot cocoa breeze that swirls through the air.

Alex and I arrived a few hours ago, only having forty five minutes to meet his parents for a quick dinner before they had to go to bed. They had to be at the church early the next morning, so they wanted to call it an early night. However, I got the impression they were using that as an excuse to hide from me. They made it abundantly clear within the first five minutes that I'm not their favorite person and that their son deserves far more than what I've got to offer. I'm not the perfect church-going girl they were expecting. Alex set me up for failure the moment he lied to them, which I didn't find out until we were at dinner and in person, sitting face to face with them.

He'd warned me beforehand that his parents were the strick, stuck-up pastor and pastor's wife duo, judgy and unforgiving with their words. Then again, that's not abnormal for Christians, especially those from a town as small as this.

Holly Grove is similar in structure to Hallow's Grove, where Alex and I live, but it's so much more festive here. The holiday spirit is embraced by the people here, and I will be the last one to complain about jolliness, even if I have to put up with Alex's parents for a few days.

They oversee the only church in town, and by the looks of their fucking massive estate, they take a hefty cut of the tithe. Almost everyone here are devout church-goers, all giving at least one-tenth of their income to the church. The wealth overflows into Alex's pocket, which benefits me, so I also can't complain about that. I'm not one to go to church anyway, so the harsh reality is that I don't care what happens to the tithe. I think it's wild that people give so much of their money to one of the most brainwashed systems.

The judgment poured from their expressions the moment their eyes locked on me. Because of what Alex told them prior to our arrival, they were expecting a quiet good girl who dresses modestly and definitely does not have bright red hair. My natural color is a light brown, but after doing a color match on myself, I knew reddish-orange was the color I was meant to live in. It brings out my best qualities, and to be honest, I look hot as fuck in it. Everyone's into the cowboy copper look these days, anyway.

I'll admit that my choice of attire probably could have been better, but I assumed Alex was being dramatic when he told me how old-fashioned they are. My blue dress has long sleeves, but it's low cut and ends on the upper half of my thigh, accompanied by translucent black tights and thigh-high boots. Yes, to the wrong crowd I may have looked a little bit like a stripper, but I thought I was in good company. I thought I'd be at least somewhat safe from judgment with Alex by my side, but I was wrong.

Completely and utterly *wrong*.

Alex hadn't come to my rescue when their perception of me became obvious. They lost even more respect for me—although I'm not sure they had any to begin with—when they began asking about the future, and I told

13

them that if Alex and I ever have kids, I don't plan on quitting my job as a hairdresser to stay home with the kids. That's not a life I've ever envisioned for myself. Sure, I don't mind kids, but they're not really my favorite, either. I've never been the motherly type, so why would I give up my career for them when I can pay a daycare to help me? Plenty of women maintain their careers these days. Having children does not have to be a death sentence to a woman's career.

"Well, you won't have much of a choice, now will you, dear? Alex's time will be consumed by the church as he prepares to take over for John, and it's your job to raise the children. You can't pay someone else to do it for you. It wouldn't be right," she'd said as I sat across from her, judgment dripping from her snippy tone.

When I began to challenge her way of thinking, Alex had stepped in, and for a split second I thought he was going to be on my side. He wrapped an arm around me, drawing me close to him, but then his poor choice of words had my jaw clenching tight.

"Sloan will do what is best for the family if the time comes," he smiled.

His mother was quick to respond. "Which will be to stay home."

I opened my mouth to protest, but Alex cut me off before I could, making me shrink back in my chair. "Correct," he nodded at his mother. "We aren't even engaged yet, so let's not get too far ahead of ourselves."

That had Grace glancing down at my bare ring finger, staring blankly at it as though she was imagining a ring on my finger, and then her lips turned down, forming a disgusted frown. She didn't hide how repulsed she was by the thought of me marrying her only son. Admittedly, I'm equally grossed out by the idea of her becoming my mother-in-law and grandmother to my future children.

Alex's father was quiet for most of the dinner, shoveling a plate full of food into his mouth, but his silence told me enough. He didn't like me either, but he couldn't bring himself to waste his breath on me, which is almost worse in some ways. That's how far I am beneath him.

After dinner, Alex and I didn't speak much. I was too hurt. How could he side with them like that? What happened to "my body, my choice"? What happened to the man who stands up for himself and doesn't let people walk all over him? Not in a million years would I have guessed that he'd bend over and be a little bitch for his parents. That's not the kind of man I want. He should have spoken up for me and stood by my side. Boyfriend or not, that's what any good person would have done. It didn't help having the people sitting around us in the restaurant listening in on our conversations. They were so invested in our exchange of words that they didn't even hesitate to avert their eyes when I'd made eye contact with them, trying to make them uncomfortable enough to look away and mind their own fucking business.

Tears welled in my eyes as we left the restaurant. I'd barely picked at my plate, feeling too nauseous and uncomfortable to eat. Grace would have probably judged me even harder if I would have eaten more than a few bites, anyway. There was no need to make it worse for myself than it already was. The guy I've been falling for over the last two months might not be the headstrong, confident guy I thought he was, and now only two or three hours into our vacation together, I'm questioning everything.

Alex keeps trying to grab my hand as we walk through downtown, but I keep rejecting his advances. I don't *want* to be touched by him right now. I'm sickened with his blatant lack of respect and inability to set clear boundaries with his parents. All I want right now is to walk through the twinkling holiday lights, take in the decorations, and forget about how horrible dinner was. And how much

16

I don't want to see his parents tomorrow. We're staying at their family cabin not far from the main house, so there's no way to avoid them. The whole point of this trip was to get to know them and become part of the family. The thought of being even remotely related to them has tears welling in my eyes again.

Small flakes of snow fall around us as we continue down the sidewalk, taking in all of the sights. I let my eyes flutter closed for a brief second as I inhale the sweet scent of peppermint hot cocoa, feeling the euphoria of holiday magic.

It's just a bad day, I remind myself. *It's not a bad life.*

It's dark now, but the town is lit up by tall poles wrapped in red and white fabric, making them look like giant candy canes. The trees lining the road are bare of leaves this late in the year, but they're covered in twinkling white lights. Downtown feels surreal, like Santa himself could stop by at any given second and give me the gift I've longed for since I was a little girl.

A love that conquers all. A lust so strong it can't be contained.

Sometimes I feel like I have that with Alex, but there are weird moments like this when I try to envision our future, and my mind draws a blank. It's like it's so far-fetched that my own imagination can't create even the slightest glimpse of what it could be.

Shaking my head, I try to get out of my own thoughts. I'm letting myself get too worked up over one bad dinner. Maybe tomorrow they'll be in a better mood and once they get to know me, perhaps they'll accept me for who I am, rather than who they want me to be. Or they'll learn to tolerate me eventually. I can live with that.

"What's your fucking problem?" Alex snaps as I pull my hand away from his for the umpteenth time.

I glance over at him, stopping in my tracks. He's never talked to me like that, and I'm not one to *let* anyone talk to me like that. "I'm sorry?" I ask, hoping I heard him wrong, but I'm pretty sure I didn't.

"How could you act like that in front of my parents? And now you won't even let me touch you. Do you know how embarrassing it is for me? The people in this town *know* who I am, and you're not even acting like you care to be here with me." There's venom laced in his low voice as his head dips toward me. He doesn't want to draw attention.

Pulling my head back, I look up at him. His eyes are dark and strained, and I almost don't recognize him. Blinking a few times before responding, I finally

18

manage to say, "It's not my fault your parents are the most uptight, ignorant people I've ever met. I didn't have a chance with them from the moment they laid their eyes on me. You said they were strict, but this is *beyond* anything I could have imagined. They're horrible people, Alex, and I did my best to stay calm. I thought I handled it better than most people would have given the situation you put me in."

Alex's voice raises slightly, making a few heads turn in our direction. "The situation *I* put you in? What fucking situation is that, Sloan?"

I narrow my eyes, shocked and in complete disbelief that he has the audacity to talk to me like this, yet he couldn't be bothered to be my voice of reason while his parents were on the attack. My tone is smooth and well-balanced as I watch him struggle to maintain control of himself. "Just because I'm not the virgin Mary herself doesn't mean I can't make you happy. I thought we've been happy, but now I don't know if any of it was real. How could you sit there and stay silent while they tore into me? What kind of man does that? You act like your parents *own* you, and it disgusts me."

Alex loses control, striking me. His hand slides across my cheek as he slaps me, forcing my head to jerk to the right. My skin was already ice cold from the frigid temperatures, making the sting of his hand hurt that much more.

My eyes are wide in disbelief as Alex stands tall, sending huffs over me with his hands now clenched into fists at his side. My jaw drops, and I suddenly have no words. It's like my brain went into overdrive and overheated, and now I'm stuck here waiting while it restarts. I've never seen him like this. He's never even come close to laying a hand on me before now, and at this moment I'm not sure one slap was enough for him. He looks like he wants to rip me in half. If looks could kill, I'd already be dead.

His medium brown eyes are bloodshot, making him look even more pale than normal. Running a hand through his disheveled dark brown hair, his fingers shake with rage. I want to step back and put space between us, but I don't want to give him the impression that he had an ounce of power over me. Holding my ground, I stare up at him, waiting for him to calm down.

Alex sees the look in my eye and tries to relax his shoulders, rolling them around while he closes his eyes and stretches his neck. He sighs loudly, releasing his clenched fists before he finally speaks. Raising his fingers to my sore cheek, he grazes them along my skin, making my bottom lip quiver with fear. "I'm so sorry I hit you," he says before meeting my eyes. "But I care so much about how they view me. They judge every aspect of my life, constantly watching my every move. I can't disappoint them. I *won't* disappoint them."

I don't respond, and instead I just listen, waiting for a better apology.

Alex continues when he realizes I have nothing to say yet. "My parents have built a name for themselves in this town, and I have to live up to it. The people here have expectations of us, and if I don't meet them, I'm out. Gone, like I never existed."

I sense there's something he's not telling me, like he's left some words unspoken, but I don't press him. Not when he's so close to losing control.

Alex wraps his arm around my shoulders, drawing my body into his. He's warm against me, yet feels so cold at the same time. His touch is the farthest thing from comfort.

Using my cold hands to push against him, I force distance between us. "I don't want you to touch me right now."

The rage ignites in his eyes once more, making me shrink back as I anticipate his next strike. Alex moves his hand like he's going to hit me again, but then a small child runs past us, screaming and laughing with his parents running behind him, yelling for him to stop. Alex's hand changes course, moving to my upper arm instead. He grips me harshly, and I'm already wondering if it'll bruise.

"You're hurting me," I hiss under my breath, remembering we can't cause a scene. Not here. Not in public like this.

Shaking my arm sharply, he elicits a whimper from me before he lets go. "Find your own way back to the cabin. I'm going for a walk, and your attitude better be *significantly* better by the time I get back," he spits before turning and walking away.

I hadn't expected to find myself trembling with tears in my eyes. This was supposed to be fun. This was *supposed* to be a bonding experience that would bring us closer.

Instead, I'm feeling lost. Broken and alone.

Chapter Two
Alex

As I storm away from Sloan, my heart pounds in my chest, rage bubbling just beneath the surface. How could she act like that in front of my parents? The embarrassment twists like a knife in my gut. I still can't believe I slapped her; I didn't want to go that far, especially somewhere people could witness it, but *fuck*, she pushed every single button I have. And all because of the situation *she* put me in—the situation I never wanted to be in.

Holly Grove is decked out in twinkling lights and cheerful decorations, the air thick with the scent of cinnamon and pine. But all I see is the petty judgment on Sloan's face and how my parents looked at her, disgust and disappointment painted across their features. They expected me to bring home the good girl, the *church* girl, who would fit into their perfect little world. But instead, I brought home a wild child with bright red hair and a sharp fucking tongue, and now I have to pay for it.

The worst part is that I'm more pissed off about Sloan than I am worried about my parents' judgment. I feel the pressure of their expectations every minute of every day—they expect me to be their perfect son. One they can be proud of and show off, one that makes the family and church look good.

By bringing her to dinner tonight, dressing the way she did, and then smacking her in the street in front of passersby, I did anything but that. It's only a matter of time before my parents find out about what happened, and I have no fucking doubt I'll hear about it.

But it's one minor slip-up. One I know I can rectify.

Sure, Sloan knows how to give good head, and the way her ass bounces on my cock is fucking mesmerizing, but I won't let my parents down. Not even for good pussy.

Fuck. All she had to do was behave for one fucking weekend. Just act the part until we can go back home. I warned her about how old-fashioned they are. About how seriously they take the church and their religion, but she didn't listen.

She never fucking does.

For whatever reason, she thought it would be appropriate to dress like a goddamn stripper headed to the club for our family dinner—what did she think was going to happen? And why the hell would she think *I* would defend her to my parents? They're *my* fucking parents. The entire dinner was a shit show, and after, well, it just got worse. How could she expect me to disappoint them and not follow in my father's footsteps? What's so wrong with staying home and raising kids? That's the wife's fucking job. Cook, clean, give me a couple of kids, and raise them while I spread the word of God. It's not that fucking hard. Shit, most women would beg for that kind of lifestyle.

But not her, of course.

I'm fucking embarrassed. *She* embarrassed me.

I reach my car, a sleek, black Mercedes-Benz S-Class, its polished exterior glimmering under the sparse streetlights, reflecting my status in this town. As the pastor's son, I'm someone people look up to, the embodiment of my family's values and the town's church. I love this life, the power it gives me, and the money that flows easily into my hands.

I lean against the car, trying to catch my breath and calm the storm brewing inside me. I need to get my head straight before I go back to the cabin. She's hurt, but she needs to understand—this is bigger than us. If she wants to be a part of my life, then she needs to meet their expectations *and* mine.

The streets are eerily quiet, the only sound the whisper of the wind and the soft crunch of snow underfoot. The town is empty at this time of night, not a soul walking the streets, and the cold seeps into my bones as snowflakes drift down from the dark sky. The sound of laughter and chatter from a nearby café echoes faintly in the background.

At least someone is having a good night.

I take a deep breath, inhaling the cold, crisp air. I can feel my phone buzzing in my pocket, and the vibrations are fucking annoying. Like a constant reminder of all the bullshit that happened tonight and all the cleaning up I'll have to do. It's probably Sloan reaching out and trying to understand what just happened. But she can wait. She needs to learn and understand that in my world, a wife doesn't get to question her husband without repercussions. That as the man in our relationship, I'll answer her when I'm good and fucking ready.

She needs to learn her place.

Something shifts in the shadows. Before I can react, I'm blindsided. The ground rushes up to meet me; the wind is knocked out of my lungs as I crash onto the snow-covered pavement. I struggle to catch my breath, but the blows keep coming, fists raining down on me fast and hard. I can barely make sense of it all—just pain and confusion as I try to defend myself. I look up, and my vision clears just enough to see the face of my twin brother, Asher.

Asher is tall—6'3", towering over me, with dark hair that falls into his eyes and tattoos snaking down his arms, each telling a story of rebellion and turmoil. As always, he's dressed in black, a uniform of defiance against everything our family stands for. The last time I saw him, he was a troubled teenager acting out in ways I never understood. My chest tightens with confusion and anger as I take in the sight of him.

What the fuck is he doing here?

"Asher? What the hell are you doing?" I gasp, wincing as he kicks me in the ribs.

Asher is the family's best-kept secret. The son that our parents made disappear to protect their image. The black sheep, the one who always fought against our parents' expectations. They tried to help him, but he just wouldn't let them, and the harder they tried, the harder he fought back. The last I heard, they sent him away to some program, hoping it would fix him, but it only pushed him further into darkness.

After that, they acted like he never existed, like he was just a ghost haunting the halls of our family home. They took down every photo and donated every single one of his belongings. They erased him from our lives like he was nothing, and all the pressure and expectations fell onto me. I had to be the perfect son, the perfect everything, all because he was too weak.

And now, here he is. The specter of everything I wanted to forget.

"Hello, twin. Didn't think you'd find me lurking out here, did you? I've been watching you, and your pathetic life is almost laughable. You're no better than them— spouting God's word while leaving their own son to fend for himself. What do you think God would say about that, huh?" His tone drips with mockery, each word a sharp dagger.

The anger boils within me, a seething fury I can barely contain. Deep down, I know he's right, and that infuriates me even more. I've played their twisted game for far too long, never daring to stand up for him because I was terrified of ending up shamed and treated like Asher. He's always struggled—whether it's a mental disability or just his chaotic wiring doesn't matter to me anymore. Instead of helping him, they punished him, shamed him, and I just watched, too cowardly to risk my own place in their precious world.

Because why would I? He never did shit for me. I didn't owe him anything then, and I sure as fuck don't now.

Their scorn echoes in my mind, a relentless reminder of the brother I lost to their impossible expectations. They always looked at him like he was too much of everything—too loud, too angry, too wild—and I hated him for it. I never wanted to be anything like him, so I played the part of the perfect son, bending to their will and molding myself into their ideal. Now, I'm left here, reaping the consequences of his refusal to fall in line.

I can't believe he's standing in front of me now, a dark cloud looming over everything. "What the hell do you want, Asher?" I snap, my voice dripping with contempt, desperate to reclaim some semblance of control in this twisted moment.

"I want to know how it feels to watch you fall apart," he growls, leaning over me, the tension in the air thickening. "You think you're living the dream, huh? You're a puppet on strings, dancing for their approval."

"Shut up," I manage to spit out, but it comes out weak, pathetic. I'm sprawled on the ground, unable to move. The world around me fades as I focus on the anger radiating off him.

He looms over me, eyes blazing with an intensity that scares me. "You do have *one* good thing, though. But, I'll treat her better than you ever could. She deserves so much more than a cowardly little bitch boy like you. It's laughable, honestly; you've had it all, Alex, and you still can't fucking get it right." He leans down, close enough for me to see the darkness in his gaze. "Maybe this Christmas, I can thank you for the early gift you gave me—the gift of showing me how family treats family."

My heart races, panic clawing at my insides. "You don't know anything about family. All you know is how to take from and use people," I hiss, trying to push myself up, but my body feels heavy, like lead.

Asher's hand slides into his pocket, and dread washes over me as I realize what he's pulling out—a knife glinting in the dim light. "What the fuck are you doing?" I shout, panic rising in my chest. "Asher, come on. You're not going to fucking kill me, cut the shit!"

But he just grins, a twisted smile that sends chills down my spine. "I think it's time for you to know what it feels like to be discarded. Just like you did to me and just like you would've done to her."

"Stop!" I plead, fear pooling in my stomach. "We can talk. We can fix this, Asher. You're my fucking brother. Let's be logical, please."

"Fix it?" he cackles, the sound echoing in the night, mocking and cruel. "You think there's anything to fix? You're just like Mom and Dad—so afraid of what I am that you'd rather pretend I don't exist."

My mind races, flashing back to our childhood. I see the two of us in the backyard, the summer sun shining down on our laughter as we play. Asher is there, his eyes bright and wild as he climbs the tallest tree in our yard, daring me to follow. I want to be just like him—to be brave and free— but I can't shake the weight of our parents' expectations. I've always been the one who follows the rules, who colors within the lines while he's always scribbled outside them, a chaotic masterpiece that nobody, not even God could ever control.

The memories hit me like a wave—how they sat me down just before starting high school, their faces drawn and serious, as they explained that Asher had to go away. They called it "help," but I felt it in my bones that they were giving up on him and tired of his chaos. I was old enough to know people around the town were talking. He was causing problems for our family and for the church, so I knew they had no other choice but to send him away.

As I grew older, I started to see Asher for what he really was—a user. He took and took from our parents, never giving back. I remember nights spent lying awake, listening to their muffled arguments about him, their anger palpable through the walls. They wanted to help him, but nothing they did helped. Shit, if anything, he just got worse.

"Get the fuck away from me," I say, desperation seeping into my voice.

Asher laughs a dark, hollow sound that echoes around us. "Don't you see, little brother—it doesn't matter what you do, you'll never be good enough. You'll never be *perfect*. Not in their eyes or the pathetic god you all bow to."

My breath quickens, panic clawing at my chest. "You're sick, Asher. You need help."

He steps even closer, the knife gleaming ominously in the moonlight. "Help? They didn't want to help me; they wanted to control me. Just like they're controlling you."

"Stop it! You don't know what you're talking about!" I shout, trying to summon some strength, but my body feels like a sack of stones.

With a surge of adrenaline, I try to push myself up, but he kicks me in the ribs, and I crash back to the ground, gasping for breath.

"Maybe this is what you need—a little reality check," he snarls, raising the knife, and I feel my heart drop.

"Please, Asher!" I scream, fear and regret flooding through me. "We can work this out! I'm sorry for how things went down, but this isn't the way!"

"Sorry doesn't cut it anymore," he sneers, his voice low and thick with contempt. He inches closer, a wicked grin curling his lips. "You really shouldn't be scared, Alex. Not if you've managed to play the perfect son, the model subject. After all, you're destined for heaven with the god you worship. But if you've let a little sin slip through your fingers…" He lets the words linger, a sinister echo in the frozen air, sending a shiver racing down my spine. "Then maybe fear is exactly what you should be feeling. What would Mommy and Daddy think? How does spending eternity with the devil sound to you?"

I swallow hard, my throat dry. His words cut deeper than the blade in his hand ever could, twisting the knife of my childhood insecurities. "Asher, don't do this," I plead, desperation clawing at my insides. "You're better than this!"

"Better?" he echoes, his laughter tinged with madness. "You think I want to be better? I'm tired of pretending, Alex. You were my brother. My fucking *twin*. If anyone was supposed to have my back, it was you, and I'm tired of you thinking you can walk away from what you've done."

The darkness closes in around us, heavy and suffocating, as if the night itself is eager to swallow me whole. My twin's twisted smile is the last thing I see before he lunges forward, the blade glinting coldly in the light. I feel a sharp, searing pain slice through my abdomen, a brutal intrusion that steals the breath from my lungs.

I gasp, a strangled cry escaping my lips, but it's drowned out by the icy wind that howls around us. My vision blurs, colors and twinkling lights swirling as I struggle to process the reality of what's happening. This can't be how it ends.

Lowering my trembling hand to my stomach, the blood seeps through my fingers, warm and sticky, contrasting against the cold. Pain radiates from the wound, sharp and consuming, like fire coursing through my veins. I can feel my strength draining away, the darkness creeping closer, pulling me under.

"Guess all those prayers didn't mean a damn thing," he sneers, his voice low and venomous. "Tell me, Alex— where's your God now?"

With those words echoing in my ears, the edges of my vision darken, and everything goes black.

Chapter Three

Sloan

I slept like absolute shit, and I spent the strong majority of the night tossing and turning while I waited for Alex to come back, but he never did. This cabin isn't insulated very well and I couldn't figure out how to get the fire started without the risk of burning down the place, so I froze while I drifted in and out of sleep.

A friendly old man from a rideshare brought me to the cabin last night after the fight Alex and I had. I knew he'd need time and space to cool off. And to be honest, I needed that too. In hindsight, it's possible that I let myself get too into my head over dinner, and that I may have directed too much of my anger at Alex when it was his parents I should have been frustrated with. I only have to see them a few times a year. If I want things to work with

Alex, I have to accept the fact that it's well within my best interest to be on good behavior and keep my lips sealed when I'm with them, even if they're assholes.

Last night as I walked through the streets of Holly Grove, I quickly noticed people staring at me, whispering amongst themselves as I passed. It was a reminder that word travels fast in these small towns. At least one person had seen Alex hit me, and now that it's the following morning, I'm sure the entire town knows.

Rolling over, I grab my phone, lighting up the screen as I tap it with my index finger. I groan, rolling my eyes when the first thing I see is a text from Alex's mom.

I expect you and Alex will meet me for lunch to discuss the altercation which occurred in town last night. We need to get ahead of it before the town has more time to change the narrative. 12:00 pm sharp - Alex knows the restaurant.

Of course, Alex knows the restaurant. There are only a handful of places to eat in Holly Grove and Alex told me most of them wouldn't pass a health inspection if the owners weren't so closely knit with the one and only inspector.

The next ten or so minutes are spent scrolling through my various social media apps and responding to

"Merry Christmas Eve" texts from friends and family. I'm already trying to mentally prepare myself for all of the engagement posts I'll see later this evening. Alex and I are nowhere near ready for a commitment that large, but a small part of me dies inside every time I see someone else from high school posting their engagement or pregnancy announcement photos. I didn't think I'd be approaching twenty eight with no engagement in sight. Most of the people I went to high school with are married with kids. I thought that would be me too, but it hasn't been in the cards for me yet.

Throwing the blankets off my legs, I shiver as the cool air rushes in around me, stealing the body heat I desperately tried to keep all night long. But I need coffee, so I sigh as I pad across the icy floors, heading straight for the cozy kitchen. It takes me a minute to find everything, but I eventually have all I need to make coffee. After pouring the dark roast grounds into the filter, I close the coffee machine up and press the button to begin the brew cycle. Steam immediately rises from the top of the tank, spitting small beads of scalding water into the air. The hot coffee begins pouring down from the drip, making my eyes instinctually flutter closed with delight, and I let my shoulders drop while I inhale the rich scent.

I *need* this. There isn't enough caffeine to get me through Christmas with Alex's family, but I'll still consume my weight in it.

A small black box placed in the center of the kitchen table catches my eye. Leaving the coffee machine, I approach it, looking around the room for Alex. I hadn't heard him come in, but this box wasn't here when I came in last night. I sat at the table for over an hour before I crawled into bed. I would have noticed it.

There's a silky onyx ribbon wrapped neatly around the matte box, making it appear luxurious. Picking it up with one hand, I glance around the room one more time before deciding to open it. The ribbon unravels easily as I pull it. Opening the lid, I find a piece of paper that has been folded and tucked inside the box. I pluck it from the box, revealing a giant wad of cash and a brass key. My eyes widen as I realize just how thick the stack of cash is. There's *easily* several thousand dollars here. Unfolding the note, I begin to read it.

Let me show you what it's like to be cherished. I have a few things to take care of before I meet you this evening, so please take this cash and spend the day shopping. Buy yourself something nice while you wait for me.

I breathe in relief as I realize this means I won't have to see Alex's mom today after all. Part of me is also relieved that I get to blow off the steam of last night with all of this cash. I've always known he has a shit load of money, but this… this is insane. And he's just telling me to go spend it like it's nothing? This doesn't make up for last night… but it helps.

When the sun goes down, our game begins. Race me to the church for midnight mass - 1043 Chestnut Avenue

The rules are simple:
1. *If I catch you once, I get to eat you.*
2. *If I catch you twice, you have to suck me.*
3. *If I catch you three times, I get to fuck you.*
4. *If I catch you three times AND get to the church before you, nothing is off-limits.*

Begin: Sundown
End: Midnight

Don't get caught.
Best of luck, my sweet doe,
A

I'm grinning from ear to ear as I reread the note a second time, and then a third. Alex must *really* feel bad about last night if he's setting up a sexy game for us to play and giving me thousands of dollars to spend on whatever I want. It sounds risky, especially considering all eyes will probably be on us today, so we'll have to be sneaky. But I suppose that's the thrill of it. What fun would it be if we didn't have to sneak around?

Alex has never been one to be spontaneous like this, but this actually sounds like a good time. I already *want* him to catch me. It's always been a fantasy of mine to play a feral game of cat and mouse, and he's making my dream come true.

Maybe he isn't such a mommy's boy after all. Perhaps he's got a darker, wild side I haven't seen yet.

God, I hope he does.

Feeling suddenly energized, I forget all about my coffee as I run to the bathroom for a quick shower and to warm up before heading out for a full day of shopping and exploring the town. It takes me well over an hour to shower, fix my hair, and throw on a face of makeup. Deciding to dress the part, I slip into a red long sleeved dress, which ends at my upper thigh. Fur-lined black boots rise over my knees, exposing my translucent black tights, which I'm hoping Alex will rip open at some point this evening.

As I head out the heavy cabin door, I slide my arms through a black overcoat and secure red and white earmuffs over my ears before they have a chance to get cold. I look and feel hot as fuck. Alex's mom will have a heart attack if she sees me like this, so I need to be extra careful.

Don't get caught, the words written on the note, replay in my mind, effortlessly sending heat between my thighs.

Today is going to be a good fucking day.

Chapter Four

Asher

The early morning air bites, sharp and cold as I watch her from the cover of the trees around the cabin. The front door creaks open, and she steps outside, her head down, clutching the note I left as if it's a lifeline. The sight pulls a dark satisfaction through me, filling me with a rush that nothing else has ever come close to. My brother may have thought he owned her, that she was part of his perfect little world, but he never knew the truth to it all—or that I've been watching.

I'd seen her first on his social media, buried under all those preppy photos he'd spam like a church newsletter. She was so easy to spot, even in a crowd, a flicker of wild in her eyes that was too bright for the stale world he was trying to drag her into. I knew then and there that she was never meant to be his.

No, she was made for *me*.

What started as harmless curiosity turned into months of watching, learning, and obsessing. The more I dug, the more I saw the parts of her he didn't. She was real and raw, and I wanted her for myself.

And now, she's mine.

She's easy to fool. The cabin they were staying in—the one Alex always bragged about, a place our parents had reserved for their perfect son—wasn't hard to get into. Just a quiet pick of the lock and a slip through the shadowy halls while she slept soundly, tucked up in the bed they would have shared. Her steady breathing filled the room, and for a moment, I just watched, taking in the calm that radiated from her, a calm I've never had and probably never will.

I stepped closer, feeling the familiar, cold pang of resentment surge into something darker, more possessive. My fingers brushed against a red lock of her hair, tucking it gently behind her ear, and I felt a twisted thrill ripple through me. This girl, so peaceful and trusting, was blissfully unaware of the storm that surrounded her, convinced she'd be meeting her perfect boyfriend in the

But the sight of the bruise blooming on her cheek—a cruel reminder of Alex's cowardice—stoked the fire within me. Rage boiled in my veins, a savage fury that twisted my gut. I'd watched him strike her, witnessed that moment of weakness, and it ignited something deep inside me. I knew, in that instant, that my twin needed to die.

He was too reckless, too pathetic to protect her. He didn't deserve her trust, her *love*.

I wanted to obliterate that worthless piece of shit once and for all, to seize everything he had and make it mine. I wanted to erase the pain he'd inflicted on her, to show her what it truly meant to be cared for—what it meant to be *mine*. I'd strip away the remnants of his abuse and mistreatment until all that was left was me, standing in the shadows, her real protector, and I'd make sure she never looked back.

So I did.

If she knew what I'd done and understood that Alex was gone, buried in the frozen ground, she'd probably never sleep again.

I pulled my hand back, curling it into a fist as a flash of memory shot through me, sharp and biting, like a frigid gust tearing through the room. The holidays never brought calm—they were a season of expectations, forced gratitude, and my father's overbearing sermons about faith and obedience.

One year, around Christmas, I slipped out during service. While Alex sang in the choir I ducked away, craving a moment alone in the biting winter cold, the fresh snow crunching under my boots as I escaped down a small path through the woods behind the church. I wanted to feel alive and free from their eyes for a few minutes, but it didn't last. I barely had ten minutes out there before my father's iron grip yanked me back inside, dragging me through the congregation's hushed, judgmental stares. I remember the glint in his eyes, that cold look as he told me I'd embarrassed the family.

That same night, after everyone else left, he let me have it. Took me out behind the cabin and belted me until my skin was raw, going on and on about how my defiance and my selfishness made me a disappointment to the family, a *stain* on his reputation as the pastor. The fury in his voice, the disgust in my mother's eyes as she watched from the window, wrapped up in her perfect, pious disappointment—that's the legacy I got. Not the approval, not the affection. Just the reminder, over and over, that I was the bad one, the unworthy one, the kid who couldn't stand still or sing the right hymns.

Afterward, they told me I had to pray for forgiveness, that God wouldn't accept a son as broken as me unless I begged. But even then, I knew they weren't talking about God; they were talking about their own twisted pride. It was always about them, never about faith, never about anything higher than their own need for control.

And now, here I am, in Alex's life, about to take his girl, in a cabin that should've been mine, with all the things they never thought I'd deserve.

She's still reading the note I left, the barely there, fake apology meticulously crafted to show her a little slice of myself, but not tip her off. Just a little bait to reel her in, to keep her from asking questions too soon. The promise of our game will keep her on her toes all day, and by the time the sun sets, she'll be practically begging for my touch.

I watch her lips move as she reads it, and a dark grin stretches across my face beneath the mask. She thinks he's ready to make amends, that he cares enough to fix this mess. Little does she know, she's merely a pawn in this game—a game I've been planning for too long. Her naivety is delicious, a sweet little morsel that only deepens my desire to claim her as my own.

My sweet doe has no idea my twin is six feet under and that I'm the only one left here.

I step back into the shadows, though I know she won't look my way. She's too wrapped up in the lie I've crafted, her mind racing with hope. She's never seen me; I doubt she even knows about me at all. This mask, this game I've set up, will be the perfect cover. She'll never know she's spending time with me, not him.

Not until it's too late.

The ski mask clings tight against my face, the fabric stretching over my skin, concealing everything but my gray eyes. I can feel the warmth of my breath inside it, mixing with the cold morning air as I stand hidden in the trees. She has no idea I'm here, watching her every move.

It's like a game—a game I know she's already lost, even if she hasn't realized it yet.

Part of me wants to skip the game all together and take what's mine, but I know I can't. This is something she needs. Something my sweet doe craves.

Right now, it's enough to watch, to keep myself out of sight until she's lulled into her usual sense of safety. I want her to look for *Alex*, to feel that twisted comfort, knowing her "perfect" boyfriend left her a sweet note and a hefty monetary gift, something to keep the lie alive.

She'll believe it's him—of course she will—until I'm ready to pull the mask off, letting her finally see who she's been playing this little game with all along. And, *fuck*, I can't wait to see her face when she realizes the truth.

Through the tangled shadows, I catch sight of her. My sweet doe striding through the woods in that damn red sweater dress, thigh-high boots with the white fur trim. She's dressed to be noticed, dressed like she's on display, like she knows she's about to be watched.

I stay in the shadows, watching her make her way through the trees.

I pull Alex's phone out, sliding my gloved fingers over the screen as I type out a quick message.

Those boots don't look like fun to run in, sweet doe.

Her phone vibrates, and I watch as she stops dead in her tracks, looking down at it with that smile of hers growing wider.

Guess I like a little challenge—think you can keep up?

Fuck, she's into it. Hooked, right where I want her. I knew she'd fall for this. It's like she's begging to be hunted, to be played with, like she wants to be chased by someone who isn't going to back down or soften up when things get dark.

Damn, if I'm not exactly what she's craving.

I've spent months learning everything there is to know about my sweet doe. Every post she's made, every picture, every pathetic, hopeful little message she's sent to Alex that he barely bothered to read—I've gone through it all. I hacked her socials, dug into the depths of her life, and found every piece she hides from everyone else. Those late-night conversations with her best friend Cara where she spills her soul, I've read it all. I know them and their friendship better than she does. Hell, I know *her* better than she knows herself.

And when she talks to Cara about what she wants, that thrill she craves that my pathetic twin hasn't been able to give her—the kind that leaves her breathless, that makes her feel alive—it's like she's calling to me, begging for someone who knows how to give her everything she wants.

She has no idea that every step she takes is leading her straight to me. My sweet doe thinks she's in control. She's still in that bubble of blissful ignorance, convinced this is all a harmless game Alex concocted just for her. But Alex was a coward, too soft and spineless to even get close to giving her what she *needs*.

But me? I've got all the patience, all the control. I've waited and watched, obsessively picking apart every little piece of her life she thought was private. Piecing together every want, every insecurity, until I knew exactly how to trap her.

Now, as I watch her from the shadows, her eager steps picking up pace as she heads toward town, I can practically feel her excitement radiating through the cold morning air.

The center of town comes into view, quiet and still, covered in a thin layer of frost that glitters under the morning light. Sloan walks right into it, her head held high, that same naive little smile on her lips. She thinks she's walking into her fairytale.

But soon enough, she'll know exactly who's waiting for her at the end of this story, and it's not her prince charming.

Chapter Five
Sloan

Holly Grove is cute, but the people here are vile. It's abundantly clear that the people here identify me as an outsider, and even more clear that they heard about what happened last night. I've done a decent job at avoiding eye contact with anyone I pass by, but the few times I've looked up, I've been met with a variety of faces. Some filled with pity, others with disgust. I don't really understand how people can be so judgmental when they weren't even there firsthand to see what happened. There were *some* people around us when we were fighting, but not *that* many.

Aside from the people, this town is really cute. The buildings are all older, but they're been taken care of and kept up quite well. Several of the paths that twist between businesses are cobblestone, adding to the holiday charm of this place. Green garland wrapped in twinkling white lights lines the front of each business downtown where the good shopping is.

Throughout the day, Alex has been sending me cryptic little messages, making me think he's watching me from afar. His note said he had a few things to take care of today, but I get the feeling I'm being watched. Every time I've turned around, fully expecting to see Alex lurking in the shadows, I'm met by nothing, which gets my excitement rising even more than when I first read his note this morning.

I spent all day shopping and exploring. I looked up the address to the church Alex gave me, and it's on the other side of town. During my venture through downtown I mentally mapped out which route I want to take when it gets dark. Without a car, it'll take me twenty five minutes to walk from here to the church. As much as I'd like to shave some of that time off by running, I don't think that's what these boots were made for, or what *I* was made for. I've never been a runner, and I don't know that I'll start tonight. Stealth will be my strategy. Plus there's snow and ice covering the entire town. The town workers did a decent job removing snow from the roads and sidewalks, but it's been snowing off and on all day, and they can't keep up with it.

"Here's your receipt," the slim, blonde cashier says from the other side of the check-out counter as she holds out the piece of paper for me to take. "Have a good evening."

"Thank you," I nod, taking the paper from her thin hand. "You, too."

Stuffing the diminished wad of cash back into my pocket, I pick up my bags and stride for the door, heading in the direction of the café I stopped at this morning. Earlier in the day I decided I'd go back for a hot chocolate before Alex and I start our game. I have a little time left to kill anyway, so this is perfect.

The icy breeze blasts my face as I step onto the snow-covered sidewalk and into the dimming daylight. My phone chimes as soon as I begin walking, prompting a grin to spread across my lips.

Alex. It has to be him.

Shuffling the bags around in my hands, I reach into my pocket for my phone. My smile widens further when I see the message on the screen.

Need some help with your bags?

I glance up from the screen, looking around the entire area. The streets are mostly empty now. Everyone has gone home to get ready for the midnight mass service. I don't know how Alex got us out of going to it tonight, but I'm fucking grateful. The thought of sitting through three hours of Alex's dad talking about shit he doesn't live by doesn't exactly appeal to me.

My fingers are hurt from the cold air as I text him back.

Yes. Are you here?

It only takes a few seconds for him to respond.

Finishing up taking care of a few things. I'm sending a car to take your bags back to the cabin. See you soon.

Shoving my phone back into my pocket, I smile to myself as I walk toward the café. The sun is on the horizon now and the temperature is dropping quickly. This game is so unlike Alex, but it suddenly feels like he's trying. Between the money, the texts throughout the day, and the fact that he put actual thought into an activity for us to do together... I feel seen. Maybe he does feel bad about what happened last night and is doing all of this because he doesn't want to lose me. Maybe it was one fuck up and won't happen again.

When I reach the café there's a black SUV waiting in front of the entrance, and there's a man dressed in a black suit patiently waiting for me.

"Miss Sloan?" he asks, his voice delightfully professional.

"Yes," I nod. "You're here for my bags?"

"I am," the man responds. "Let me take those for you. They'll be waiting for you in the cabin."

He stretches his arms out, gently taking the load of bags off my arms. The relief from the loss of all that weight is instant, making me roll my shoulders and neck around.

"Thank you," I smile as he loads them into the SUV.

"Is there anything else I can assist you with before I leave, Miss Sloan?" he inquires, turning to fully face me with his hands clasped behind his back.

"No," I shake my head. "You're done more than enough. I think I'll warm up in the café before meeting with Alex."

"Have a good evening," the man smiles before getting back into the SUV and driving off with my bags.

Turning back toward the café, I feel weirdly taken care of. I didn't even have to tell Alex that I had too many bags and didn't want to walk around with them all night. He just *knew* what I needed and acted on it. It's a different side of him, and I'm hoping it's here to stay.

Several unfamiliar faces turn to stare at me as I enter the café, but I ignore them as I quickly find an empty table. A waitress wastes little time approaching my table.

"What can I get for you?" she asks as she smacks a piece of gum between her teeth. She doesn't look up at me as she waits for my response, holding a pen and paper between her fingers.

"Just a hot chocolate, please," I smile up at her.

Her eyes flick to mine, annoyance clear in them. "That all?"

"Yes," I nod, tapping my fingers on the top of the table. "I won't be staying long."

"Alright," she sighs, shoving the pen and paper back in her apron before she disappears into the kitchen.

I risk a glance around the café to find multiple people still staring at me. They're not even trying to hide it, and I think that's what annoys me most. If my best friend Cara were here, she'd be telling them to go fuck themselves. She'd scare the shit out of them enough to make sure they didn't so much as think about looking in my direction.

Rolling my eyes, I force myself to carry on and shove them to the back of my mind.

The church is on the other side of town and so many of the streets look similar, especially when the entire town is covered in snow. Pulling up my map on my phone again, I try to memorize the route I'm going to take. I tried to throw a few weird twists in there, something to throw Alex off and give me more time before he finds me.

Although, I'm definitely hoping he *does* catch me. But I don't want to play easy to get. This is going to be the sexiest game of cat and mouse anyone has ever played, and I can't think of a more taboo place to play it. If anyone catches us, word will spread through the town like wildfire, ten times faster than what they saw last night.

Alex's parents would have a fucking heart attack. They'd never let us live it down. We'd probably be shunned from Holly Grove forever. Then again, that may not be the worst thing in the world.

The impatient waitress returns to my table with a steaming mug of hot chocolate, topped with whipped cream and a pinch of peppermint flakes. I give it a minute to cool down before bringing it to my lips, and when I do, I melt into the mug instantly. The warmth fills me, heating me to my core. This is exactly what I needed before I take off into the night, fleeing for the church.

Tights might not have been the smartest choice on such a cold night, but I know it'll heat things up quickly when Alex tears through them to gain access to my body.

I sip my hot chocolate until it's completely dark outside, and then I throw a one hundred dollar bill onto the table as I stand to leave. The waitress certainly doesn't deserve it because of her attitude, but it is Christmas Eve and I'm sure she can use it. It's not my money anyway, so it feels like the right thing to do.

Pulling my overcoat tightly around my body, I step through the café doors and into the snowy night, excited and already feeling the pulsing heat as it builds between my thighs.

Chapter Six
Asher

She doesn't see me, but I see her. *Always.* Every step she takes, every little decision—like the handfuls of bags she carried around before I sent Jacobs, one of the family's drivers, to retrieve them. She did what I told her and used the cash I left her to treat herself.

Good.

I *want* to spoil her, to give her everything she's ever been denied. Alex never fucking got it. He never cared enough to notice the little things, or the way she lights up when she feels appreciated. He treated her like some accessory, something to show off when it suited him.

My brother was fucking pathetic.

But me? I'll show her what it's like to be cherished, adored, *owned.* She doesn't know it yet, but her life already belongs to me. I'd burn this whole fucking town to the ground if it meant making her happy and putting a smile on her pretty little face.

She slows at a crosswalk, her breath curling in the cold evening air, and my pulse quickens. Soon, my sweet doe will see the difference. My brother failed her, but I fucking won't.

Moving through the busy downtown, I shadow her from a distance, keeping my steps light and steady, hidden by the flow of people coming and going behind me. Their boots crunch over patches of ice and snow as they shuffle about.

Holly Grove has always been a tourist town. For as long as I can remember, people traveled from around the world to hit the infamous slopes. To them, there is no better way to spend the holidays. Little do they know, everything about this stupid town and its people is fake. They're not the warm, welcoming townsfolk you'd expect to find. No, this town is filled with judgmental assholes who turn on their own and anyone else who dares to be different from them.

Anyone who doesn't share their beliefs or morals.

The people passing by are all wrapped up and half-hidden in their bundles of winter clothing, meaning Sloan won't even think twice if she happens to catch a glance at me. I blend in with the crowd like another passerby caught in the season's chill.

I'm just part of the fucking scenery—until I decide otherwise.

Not that I'm worried. My sweet doe doesn't see me; she doesn't even *sense* me. And that's the beauty of this little game I've created.

She stops to check her phone, oblivious to how I'm closing in with each second that ticks by. She's fucking beautiful like this—unsuspecting, wrapped in a red sweater dress that hugs her just right. Her gaze drifts from shop to shop as if in search of the precious boyfriend she thinks set up this little game for her.

Wrong again, sweet doe.

Tucking her phone in her pocket, she continues down the snowy lane. I bite my lip beneath my thick wool ski mask, watching the way her hips sway as she walks, each step giving me a perfect view of her plump ass jiggling just enough to make my mouth water. I'm only a few steps behind, savoring it, every part of me itching to sink my teeth into that warm, soft flesh to mark her as mine.

Icicles hang from the eaves outside the shops, catching in the yellow light of lamp posts while snowflakes drift lazily from the darkening sky, settling on the hats and scarves of tourists shuffling by amid their last-minute shopping. I track her silently, inhaling when the wind shifts, welcoming her scent as it hits my nose—a mix of amber and something sweetly wild.

Fuck. She's warm even in the freezing air, and her scent lingers long after she's walked through like she's unknowingly marked a path for me. Every street she crosses and every alley she considers turning down leads exactly where I want her—I've made sure of it.

There's only one path for my sweet doe to take, and I can already feel the thrill building as I watch her unknowingly walk right into my trap. The hunter in me savors every moment, anticipating the sweet satisfaction of watching her become my prey, helpless and bound to me.

There was a time when I loved this town and its people. It was home once, full of familiar faces, comfort, and laughter. But that was before they turned on me, before they looked at me with the same disapproval my parents did simply for being different. Before they cast me out and were more than willing to go along with my parents, pretending I never existed.

Now, I see them for what they really are: a town full of fucking cowards and sheep who sneer and gawk from a safe distance. They judge with their eyes, condemning anyone who doesn't fit into their perfect little world or bow down to their silent god.

Every single piece of shit in this town is worthless to me—except for her.

She rounds the corner, and I follow without a sound, my pulse picking up as she turns into the narrow alley behind Sugar & Spice Bakery. I already knew she would take this route. It's exactly as I had planned. A few steps more, and she'll be right where I want her.

This alley is a dead end, it's why I chose this one. She pauses, glancing around before realizing the way she turned leads nowhere. I watch as her shoulders tense, waiting, my eyes locked and waiting for the perfect moment. She hesitates and finally turns around.

And then I make my move.

In a single, fluid step, I'm there—my body crashing into hers, pinning her against the cold brick wall with a satisfying thud. My hands brace her shoulders, my presence close enough to catch the startled gasp that slips from her lips. The way her body tenses at first, then slowly softens, tells me everything I need to know.

My sweet fucking doe thinks I'm him. *Alex*.

She sighs—just a little—like she's melting into me, and I feel her trust, raw and blind. She has no idea that I'm not my brother, but I can feel the way her heartbeat skips beneath my palms, hear her breath hitch as she leans into me, all too willing. She doesn't fight; she doesn't even pull away. No, instead, she presses closer, like she's been waiting for this moment, for *him*.

Her lips part, and I can taste the air between us, thick with her need. A soft smile tugs at her lips as she whispers, her voice almost tentative, "Alex…"

I could fucking laugh. The sound almost bursts out of me, but instead, I let her have this illusion. I let her believe in the lie a little longer. She relaxes, sinking further against me, like I've unlocked something deep inside her. The words she breathes send a charge straight to my cock, pulling me in deeper, urging me to take what I want.

She's already fucking mine.

Leaning in closer, I let her feel the heat radiating off me and the tension that crackles in the space between us. Her body presses against mine, soft and trembling. The way she moves beneath me is fucking maddening; she's so unaware of the storm she's invited by playing my little game. To think *he* had her like this for so long… It makes my blood boil. He didn't fucking deserve her, not like this. He never knew how to take care of her, how to make her burn.

But I do.

She looks up at me, her gaze so trusting, it's almost fucking cute. She has no idea. Her hands reach up, brushing over my chest, before hooking into the straps of my vest and pulling me in closer like she needs me—like I'm what she's been *craving*.

Behind my mask, a smirk forms on my lips as I gently lift the bottom part of it up, exposing my chin and lips to the cool winter air. I lean in, my lips brushing against the soft skin of her neck, and she shudders with the contact.

She melts into me, her breath quickening, her pulse fluttering like it wants to break free. Every soft kiss or nip I leave along her jawline, every touch—it's like she's unraveling in my hands, and fuck if I don't love it.

Her pouty lips part, and I can hear a soft sigh escape her, I can feel the way her body tenses when she whispers his name. "Oh, fuck, Alex…"

Fuck, this is too good. It's good enough to have my cock rock hard, throbbing to sink itself inside her. This is just the beginning. Tonight, I'm going to fucking ruin her, and my sweet doe is begging for it without even knowing.

I press closer, our bodies flush against each other, and when she gasps, I can taste her need. Her hands clutch at me tighter, her nails digging into my tactical vest like she's trying to hold onto something intangible, trying to find stability in this chaos.

But there's no stability here, not anymore. Not when I'm the fucking one she's falling into.

I pull her in, my mouth tracing her jawline, feeling every tremble she can't control.

She whispers again, the heat in her voice unmistakable. "When did you get so good at this?"

I feel a sick thrill at the words. *This?* Shit, my brother was slacking if she thinks *this* is good. She has no idea what I have in store. This is only round one, and I haven't even fucking started. I know what she wants—what she needs—and now that my twin is out of the way, I'm the one who's going to give it to her.

Not him. Not *Alex.*

I lower my lips to her neck again, letting my teeth graze her chilled skin. She gasps, her head tilting back, and at that moment, when I see her eyes roll back, I know I fucking own her.

There's no going back for her now. She's all fucking mine.

I bite back a smirk, savoring the secret as long as I can. The way she expects him, but she's getting me—the better version. Fuck, I can't wait to see the look on her face.

I let my hands wander, sliding lower until I find the curve of her hips. I pull her flush against me just enough to feel her breath catch. It's intoxicating, watching her lose herself in her own carnal need.

I can feel her heart pounding against me, hear the uneven breaths escaping her lips as I slide a hand up her leg, slowly and teasingly, feeling the heat of her through the fabric of her dress.

She's ready.

I drop to my knees in the snow in front of her, not giving her any time to react, not letting her question what's happening. I look up at her through my mask, catching her gaze for just a second before I force her legs apart and shove her dress up her thighs.

"Oh shit," she gasps, her head falling back against the brick wall as her hands find their way to my shoulders.

She's soft and pliant, and I can instantly see just how fucking wet my sweet doe is for me. Her body is quivering like it can't decide whether to fight or surrender, and I can't help but smirk.

"Shh, sweet doe. You know the rules," I add, keeping my tone dark.

Her breath catches when I pull her closer and run my tongue up the see through tights covering the inside of her thigh, tasting her sweat-coated skin and savoring the sweetness of her.

Damn. She is easily going to be the sweetest thing I've ever tasted.

Without hesitation, I bunch the delicate see-through fabric in my fists. The sound of the tear is violent, almost as jagged as the thoughts clawing around inside my head. Her flawless skin appears beneath the ruined fabric. My chest tightens, my breath coming in ragged and uneven as I pull the pieces apart, baring more of her to me.

She groans, her body freezing as I glide my hot, slick tongue across her soaked center.

"Jesus Christ," she moans with panted breath, using a hand to brace herself against the wall.

Smirking, I brush my fingers along the folds of her pussy. My gaze finds hers again as I teasingly flick my tongue against her clit, just enough to drive her crazy before I pull back.

"Fucking hell," I mutter under my breath, the taste of her driving me insane. "You don't even know how fucking good you taste."

I don't give her a chance to respond—my patience has long run dry, and gentleness is not on the table. I run my tongue across her slickness again. Lapping, licking and sucking at her sensitive flesh, claiming every inch of her with a possessive hunger as my fingers part her, holding her open for me. The sweet taste of her consumes me, and I savor it, drawing her to the edge of madness. Her moan breaks the silence of the alley, raw and unrestrained, and I feel it go straight to my hardening cock. She arches, pressing into the cold wall, as her body instinctively shies away from the heat of my tongue.

"Fuck, Alex. Yes—" Her voice cracks, breathless, but the words die in her throat as I flick my tongue over her again, teasing, devouring.

Slowly, I slide two fingers inside her, following the rhythm of my mouth, slow, deliberate, but insistent. Each stroke, each *press*, has her crying out. Gripping the wall and my shoulder for support as I force her to take it, to surrender completely to me.

Her legs tremble; every shudder from her is just another signal for me to push her harder. I slip another finger inside, stretching her, and I hear her gasp—a sound that drives me to the edge of madness myself.

Fuck. She's already lost, and I'm the one who's taking her. Not *him*.

I growl against her skin, pulling her closer. "Don't you fucking pull away," I rasp, my voice low, dark. "This is only round one, baby. And I'm not done with you yet. I caught you, my sweet doe, and you will let me have my prize."

Her fingers tangle in the fabric of my ski mask, pulling me deeper between her legs as she guides me right where she wants me; little does she know, she's not the one in control.

No, I'm in charge here.

I pull back just enough to flick my tongue over her clit again, but this time, I do something different. I sprinkle snow onto my tongue, feeling the cold bite against my mouth before I return to her. The instant shock of it against her sensitive pussy has her body jerking, her back arching as the cold slices through her, and I watch with a satisfied smirk as she flinches.

She gasps, her hands pushing weakly against my shoulders, but I don't let her move. "W-what the hell?" Her voice trembles, but it's nothing more than a desperate plea.

I growl, my grip tightening on her hips, holding her firmly in place. "Don't pretend you don't like it," I snap, my voice rough and commanding, the dark edge of hunger dripping from every word. "Besides, I won this round, sweet doe. Not you." I press my cold tongue deeper into her, forcing her to take it, forcing her to feel the bite of ice against her warmth. I watch her shudder, her legs trembling, but there's no denying her arousal as she melts into it.

Into *me*.

"You'll fucking take whatever I give you," I growl, my voice a primal rasp, teeth grazing her skin as I push harder, relentlessly as my fingers pump in and out of her. "You're such a good little slut for me, aren't you? Come on, I want to hear you beg for it."

She's quivering, trying to hold back the moans, but she can't. She's already unraveling, caught in the tension I've built between us. The suspense. Every breath she takes, every shudder, tells me exactly how far gone she is.

"This Christmas, you're going to give me the only gift I desire. You're going to fucking break for me," I whisper, the words dark, filled with a raw hunger as my fingers match the feverish pace of my mouth. She's so close now, trembling with anticipation, ready to shatter under me. I feel it in every inch of her—her surrender is coming, and I'm going to make her want it.

"Please…" she breathes out, her voice shaky, desperate. "I'm so close…"

I push her closer to the edge, feeling her body quiver harder as I go deeper, faster. The sounds she's making— soft gasps, desperate pleas—only push me further into a frenzy. And when she finally falls apart, her body shuddering, gasping my dead brother's name, I feel a dark satisfaction settle deep in my chest.

"Oh my god, Alex—" she gasps, her voice vibrating, thick with desperation and panic, like she's lost in the moment, completely fucking undone.

She doesn't even know it, but she's calling for me.

"That's it, sweet doe," I growl, my voice thick and rough, dripping with satisfaction and a twisted sense of ownership. It's low and dark, like a predator savoring the moment before the kill. "Fucking break for me."

Her body shudders, pussy clenching around my fingers as she unravels, and I can't help but smile—this is my victory, my mark on her. But there's something else gnawing at me, something darker. I hope Alex saw every fucking second of it. I hope he watched as his precious

Sloan came on his sinner of a brother's tongue. I want him to rot in hell knowing that she's mine now—owned, used, broken.

I pull back slowly, the warmth of her still lingering on my tongue as I slide my fingers out of her and pull her dress back down, smoothing the fabric over her still quivering body. My fingers linger on the hem for a moment, just enough to send a shiver down her spine.

"Run," I command, my voice now cold and sharp, starkly contrasting the heat still pulsing between us. "I'll give you a ten-second head start,"

She's panting, disoriented, her legs shaking as she struggles to regain some control. But I won't wait. I stand up straight, watching her, daring her to make a move. "Go," I repeat, darker this time, the command carrying more weight than she can ignore. "Because round two just started."

Chapter Seven

Sloan

My feet pound against the snow-covered sidewalk, each step sending little explosions of white powder into the air. My breath comes in quick, visible cloud puffs, but I can't tell if it's from running or from what just happened with Alex. The streetlights cast long shadows that dance and twist with every movement as I flee through the streets.

Holy. Fucking. Shit.

The memory of his mouth on me, right there in the open, makes me stumble. I catch myself on a lamppost, its yellow light casting a warm aura in the darkness around me. My legs are shuddering — from the wintry air, from moving them harder than I have in months, from *him*. I press my forehead against the cool metal of the lamppost trying to catch my breath, trying to process what just happened.

That wasn't the Alex I know. Not the Alex who carefully straightens his tie before every business meeting, who measures his words like precious gems before letting them fall from his lips. Not the Alex who calculates every risk, who plans ten steps ahead like he's playing some elaborate chess game with the world. No, the man who just had me against that wall was something else entirely. Something darker. Wilder and more feral.

Something I want *more* of.

Need more of.

I close my eyes, and immediately I'm back there – his hands gripping my hips hard enough to bruise, his mouth hot and demanding against my pussy. The way he growled—actually *growled*—when I tried to push him away. The sound still echoes in my ears, primal and possessive. It should have scared me. Instead, it lit me up from the inside out, like he'd struck a match in my soul.

I push off from the lamppost and start running again, my black boots crunching through fresh snow. The streets are quiet. Everyone else is inside the church for the midnight mass service by now. The cold air feels good against my flushed skin, and I need to move, *need* to do wouldn't have to run again and he'd be throat fucking me with his dick so hard I'd see stars instead of snowflakes. The thought sends a shiver down my spine that has nothing to do with the temperature. What else is he hiding behind that perfectly controlled facade? What other delicious darkness is he keeping locked away?

A car passes by, its headlights momentarily illuminating the empty street, making the falling snow look like stardust. I check my phone – still two hours until the game ends. Plenty of time to get there, even with the snow falling harder.

Glancing around, I'm not entirely sure where I'm at. Pulling out my phone again, I try to pull up my maps, but I don't have enough service to get it to work.

"Fuck," I curse under my breath.

The snow has transformed the little town into something even more dreamlike. The buildings are getting harder to see through the thickening snowflakes, but the twinkling holiday lights are like magic as they illuminate the copious amounts of holiday decor scattered throughout the streets.

My mind wanders back to Alex as I get lost in the falling flakes. He transformed into something unfamiliar. Something that makes me ache in places I didn't know could ache. Places that still pulse with the memory of his touch, his teeth.

God, his *teeth*.

The thought of his teeth makes me press my thighs together as I force myself to walk, trying to ease the ache that's building again. The way he scraped them across the most sensitive parts of me... *Fuck*.

If he could be like this all the time... God, maybe I *could* handle his parents' constant judgment, their unveiled disapproval. Maybe I could deal with his mom's passive-aggressive comments about my background and her blatant remarks about other women from "good families." Perhaps I could stomach his father's dismissive glances, the way he looks at me like I'm some temporary amusement his son will eventually outgrow.

Because that version of Alex? The one who grabbed me like he'd die if he didn't taste me right that second? That version doesn't give a fuck about any of it. That version would probably bend me over his mother's precious marble countertops without a second thought.

The image hits me so hard I have to stop walking for a moment, bracing myself against a brick wall. The rough texture grounds me, helps me focus on something other than the heat pooling low in my stomach. Snow melts against my ungloved hands, but I barely notice the cold. All I can feel is the memory of his tongue on my pussy.

I push off from the wall and keep moving, my boots leaving a trail of footprints that's already being erased by fresh snow. The wind is picking up, carrying away the sweet scent of Holly Grove. Somewhere in the distance the church bell rings, the sound muffled by the falling snow. The service is over and people will be flooding the streets soon. Midnight mass is over by now and they'll be going out for hot cocoa and Christmas Eve festivities before returning home for the night.

He's still out here, stalking me. The thought alone makes my heart race faster. Is he as worked up as I am? Is he thinking about what just happened, about how we *both* lost control? Or has he already regained his composure, already locked that wild animal back in its cage?

God, I hope not.

I round another corner, realizing I've wandered into an even more unfamiliar part of town. The buildings here are older, their windows dark except for the occasional Christmas light display. The storefronts have a slightly shabby charm—a used bookstore with frost-edged windows, a vintage clothing shop with mannequins draped in velvet and lace, a tiny café with chairs stacked on tables visible through the glass.

Two guys are standing beneath the café's awning, sharing a cigarette. They notice me immediately—of course they do. I'm the only other person crazy enough to be out in this weather. The ember of their shared cigarette glows bright orange in the darkness, like a tiny warning beacon, but I ignore it.

"Excuse me," I call out, already regretting the decision as their eyes rake over me. One tall and lean, the other shorter but broad, both wearing leather jackets despite the cold. "Can you point me toward the church?"

The taller one takes a long drag of his cigarette, smoke curling from his lips as his thin lips curve into a smile. His teeth are sharply white against the darkness. "Sure thing, sweetheart. You lost?"

"Just turned around in the snow," I say, keeping my distance. But the shorter one closes it anyway, stepping forward until I can smell the cigarette smoke clinging to his jacket, mixed with something sweeter—whiskey, maybe.

"It's dangerous for a pretty thing like you to be out alone this late," he says, reaching out to touch my waist. I step back quickly, but his hand follows, fingers grazing the soft fabric of my coat. His touch is nothing like Alex's—where Alex burned, this man's touch leaves an uneasy wave of chills jolting through my body.

"You should let us walk you there," the taller one adds, his smile growing wider as he flicks ash into the snow. "Keep you safe, you know?"

"I'm good, thanks." I take another step back, but my mind isn't really here with these two. It's back with Alex, wondering how far behind me he is. Wondering what he'd do if he saw another man's hands on me right now. The thought sends another shiver through me—half fear, half something else entirely. "Just point me in the right direction." My voice is flat and firm.

The shorter one holds up his hands in mock surrender, but his eyes are still undressing me. I can feel them like phantom touches, making my skin crawl. Raising his finger and pointing, he says, "Three blocks that way, then left for two more. Can't miss it."

I'm already walking away before he finishes speaking, their muttered comments fading into the snowy night behind me. Something about "stuck up bitch" and "her loss," but I don't care enough to make out the rest.

Let them look. *Let* them want. They don't matter. *None* of it matters.

Because somewhere in this snow-covered town, Alex is hunting me. And maybe, just maybe, I want to be caught. I *want* to see what's going to happen when he forces me to my knees in the snow. I want to find out just how dark his darkness goes.

I pick up my pace, snow crunching beneath my feet. My heart is pounding again, but not from fear. From anticipation. From the endless possibilities of what he'll do to me in an empty church on Christmas Eve night.

From knowing that something has shifted tonight, irreversibly. That we've crossed some invisible line, and there's no going back.

And God help me, I don't want to go back. I want to *run* forward, full speed, into whatever storm is coming.

Into his darkness.

Chapter Eight

Asher

I watch her walk away, her hips swaying in that way that makes my blood run hot. She doesn't even realize the two assholes under the café's awning are practically drooling over her. My fists clench at my sides as I catch their murmured comments. They're not subtle. Not even close. And when that tall fuck touched her?

I'm still trying to stop myself from fucking his shit up right here and now.

Then they look at each other, a silent exchange passing between them like they're wolves who've just spotted wounded prey. The taller one tosses his cigarette into the snow and nods toward Sloan. My heart pounds, the heat in my veins turning into a cold, sharp rage as they step off the curb and start following her.

Like fuck.

I trail them, my boots crunching softly against the snow. They're too focused on Sloan to notice me—*fucking amateurs.*

The taller one laughs under his breath, his voice low and lecherous as he mutters something I don't quite catch. The shorter one, Marcus, makes some crude comment about her ass, and that's all it takes for me to see red.

Marcus. I know him—everyone around here does. The sleazy little punk with the smug smile who thinks he's untouchable. I've seen the social media posts about him, the whispers on local forums, the headlines that everyone pretends to forget. Accusations of rape. Multiple women came forward, but nothing ever stuck. His parents' money kept his name clean, but I know the truth. Everyone does.

And now, this piece of shit thinks he can follow Sloan?

Not if I have anything to say about it.

I follow them for a block, staying far enough back to avoid their notice. The ski mask I slipped on earlier hides my face, but the cold air bites at the sliver of skin it doesn't cover. Sloan is still ahead, oblivious, her red hair catching the glow of the holiday lights like fire in the snow.

She's so fucking beautiful it hurts. These bastards don't even deserve to *look* at her.

Marcus nudges the taller guy, his voice carrying just enough for me to catch. "Bet she's got a tight little—"

My hands curl into fists.

The taller one laughs again. "Think she's alone?"

Marcus smirks. "Guess we'll find out."

I stop walking. My breath fogs the air as I take a moment to calm the fire raging in my chest. They don't see me yet, too busy watching Sloan's every movement like the predators that they are to even notice they're being hunted themselves.

Big mistake.

Marcus doesn't know it, but he just signed his fucking death warrant.

Traffic snarls ahead, a long line of cars stalled at a stoplight beside the wooded park, its paths lined with Christmas inflatables and strings of twinkling lights. The air smells of pine and frost, the faint jingle of a holiday tune drifting from the speakers mounted somewhere out of sight. Sloan crosses the street quickly, her figure illuminated for a moment in the glow of a giant inflatable Santa before she disappears down the snow-dusted sidewalk.

The two dipshits aren't so lucky. They pause at the curb, their pace faltering as they glance around, trying to spot where she went. The taller one mutters something under his breath, looking annoyed, while Marcus flashes his typical cocky grin, clearly confident they'll catch up.

They won't.

I trail them as they veer off the main path, following the winding walkway into the wooded park. The lights stretch ahead, a kaleidoscope of reds, greens, and whites reflecting off the snow, casting the trees in an eerie, shifting glow. The inflatables—everything from grinning snowmen to a reindeer in a rocking chair—sway slightly in the frigid wind, their movements almost lifelike in the flickering light.

The further in we go, the quieter it becomes. The festive music fades, replaced by the crunch of snow under boots and the occasional rustle of branches overhead. Everyone else has gone home, tucked away with their families for Christmas Eve. The park feels deserted, the kind of empty that sends a shiver up your spine.

They pass a towering nutcracker standing guard at the edge of the pond, its painted face frozen in a hollow grin. The pond itself glistens under the lights, its surface frozen and slick, surrounded by a low metal railing. Sloan's long gone now, but these idiots aren't giving up. Marcus nudges the taller one, his voice low but audible as he laughs, probably cracking some dumb joke about catching up to her.

I hang back, my boots soundless in the snow as I slip between the inflatables, keeping to the shadows.

They stop near the edge of the pond, scanning the area. The taller one curses again, kicking at the snow in frustration, while Marcus shoves his hands into his pockets, his grin never faltering. I see his breath puff out in little clouds, his confidence radiating off him like a stink.

He doesn't know I'm here.

Stepping out from behind a trio of inflatable penguins, I move toward them, silent as a wolf closing in.

They don't see me until I'm too close.

"Lose something?" I ask, my voice low, sharp, and cutting through the cold air like a blade.

They turn around, startled, but they're quick to cover it up. The taller one sneers, his jaw tightening as he sizes me up. "Who the fuck are you?"

Marcus, cocky as hell, steps forward. The idiot's trying to play it off like I'm just some pissed-off bystander, not someone who knows exactly what they've been doing.

"You're really following us, man?" he sneers, folding his arms. "What? You think you're some kinda hero? This isn't your fight."

I let out a low chuckle, the kind that doesn't reach my eyes. "You two were so fucking worried about chasing tail you'll never touch, you didn't even notice I've been trailing you since the café," I say, the words laced with venom. I take another step forward, my presence closing in on them. "You think you're slick? That you're low-key? Idiots. I saw every move you made, heard every fucking word that slipped from your disgusting mouths."

The taller one snorts, his chest puffing up, trying to act like he's not rattled. "Yeah? And what? You think you're some big bad hero now, huh? You're just another fucking punk hiding behind a mask. I don't see a cape, do you?"

Marcus laughs, his grin twisted with arrogance. "Oh shit, you've been following us? What? Are you trying to play protector? Get over yourself, man. We're just having some fun. Don't make it more than it is." He leans in, throwing a mocking glance at me. "You're really gonna try and play the tough guy in front of us? Cute."

I sneer at them, the words dripping with disdain. "Of course you would think you can just take whatever you want. *Touch* whatever you feel like; I'm sure your mommy and daddy raised you to be just like that. Because the world didn't have enough entitled pieces of shit. Well, you're in my world now, and in my world, the villain's the one you need to fear, not the hero."

Marcus looks at me like I'm the one in the wrong, like I'm ruining his fun. "Fuck you, man. What's it matter to you? If it's that big of a deal you can have her when we've both—"

I don't give him a chance to finish. Before he can blink, I'm on him, grabbing him by the throat and slamming him into the metal railing by the pond. His head hits with a satisfying crack, and he wheezes as I tighten my grip, pushing him harder into the cold iron.

"You think you can talk like that about her?" I growl, my voice dark and thick with rage. "Think you can follow her around like some fucking animal and then touch her? You're nothing but a filthy piece of shit."

His hands claw at my wrist, gasping for air, but he can't get free. The taller guy hesitates, taking a step forward, but I don't even look at him. Instead, I pull the knife from my pocket, flashing it in the dim light. It catches the glow of the Christmas lights, the blade wicked and cold. The coward freezes in place.

"You want a turn?" I ask, my tone cold, barely glancing at him. "One more step, and I'll carve you open like a Christmas turkey."

He swallows hard and backs off, terrified. That's what I thought.

Marcus, though, doesn't learn his lesson. "You think this makes you tough?" he manages, his voice hoarse and weak. "You don't even know her. You're just some wannabe tough guy, trying to play pretend."

I can't help but laugh. It's bitter and filled with venom. "Tough guy? You think I'm playing some kind of game here? I don't need to 'play' anything. I'm just pissed off that I have to waste my time on assholes like you."

I slam him against the railing again, harder this time. His eyes bulge in panic, and I can feel his body go limp in my grip. He can't handle this. None of these creeps ever can.

"You think I don't know who you are?" I spit, my words dripping with contempt. "Marcus fucking Keller. The rich little prick who thinks he can do whatever the fuck he wants. Where's your daddy's money now, though, huh? It can't fucking save you. Not from me."

His eyes flicker with fear, his bravado slipping away. "I—I didn't mean it," he gasps, choking. "It was just a joke, man. We didn't mean to—"

I cut him off by slamming him into the railing again, this time with everything I've got. His head bounces off the cold steel, and I can feel the rage surge in me. "A joke? You think this is funny?" I spit on the ground. "You think it's funny to follow her? To plan to touch her like she's some fucking toy for you to use at your convenience?"

His lips quiver, but he's too fucking scared to speak. His hands paw uselessly at my wrist, and I'm not done yet.

"Hey, man, chill," his friend starts, raising his hands. "We didn't mean anything by it."

"Shut the fuck up." I snap my head toward him, and he freezes. "You've got five seconds to walk away before I take that fucking cigarette and shove it so far down your throat you choke on it."

He doesn't need to be told twice. He bolts, slipping on the snow as he disappears into the woods, leaving his friend to fend for himself.

Marcus continues struggling under my grip, his breath coming out in panicked, shallow gasps. He tries to fight, squirming, but the icy railing cuts into his back as he pushes against it, his hands slapping uselessly at my forearm.

"You're not going anywhere," I growl, my voice low and dangerous. I press harder, watching as fear floods his eyes. His bravado is gone, replaced with the realization that he's not in control anymore. Not now, not *ever*.

"Come on, man," he stammers, his voice cracking. "We weren't gonna do anything, I swear."

"Do I look like I believe you?" I press the knife against his throat, hard enough to make him wince. "You're a fucking joke, Marcus. Always were. Following other people around like a lost dog, begging for scraps. You think that makes you a man? You think that makes you good enough to even look at her?"

"She's just some stupid bitch, man. A fucking tourist!" he blurts out, panic flooding his voice. "She'd have been gone after the holiday, no harm done."

I don't waste a second. Grabbing him by the collar, I drag him off the railing, throwing him down onto the frozen pond with a sickening thud. The moment his body hits the ice, it cracks beneath us, the sound like thunder in the dead of night. His yelp is drowned out by the groaning of the ice as it starts to split and fracture.

"You're fucking crazy!" he yells, his voice high and panicked.

"Crazy enough to make sure you never see Christmas morning."

The ice beneath us shatters, sharp and sudden, the sound ringing in the air like a death knell. Marcus's eyes go wide as the surface gives way, the frozen water splitting open, and he plunges in with a panicked scream. I don't move. I stab my knife into the ice, driving it deep, watching as it splits further, the cracks spreading fast, like a spider's web about to collapse.

Marcus flails in the freezing water, trying to claw his way back to the surface. I stand firm, watching him struggle. Beneath the ice is brutal, violent—there's no escape.

He clings to the edge of the ice, gasping for air, his face contorted with desperation. I step closer, my boots crunching on the brittle surface as I kneel, towering over him. I look down at him with nothing but hatred, the weight of my presence pushing down on him like an unrelenting force.

"You wanted to mess with her?" I sneer, my voice cold, taunting. "Thought you could just play with a girl like her, huh? Just another tourist to use and throw away?" I pull my knife from the ice, the blade gleaming in the dim light, and without hesitation, I drive it into his hand, pinning him to the ice with a sickening twist.

His scream is muffled, his fingers curling around the hilt of the knife, but I don't care. His pain is nothing compared to what he deserves.

I mutter, shaking my head in mock pity. "Well, look where that got you. Ironic, isn't it? Now, I'm the one who gets to have all the fun. I'm the one who gets to fucking mess with you, and guess what, Marcus, when I'm done, I get to throw you away, too."

I let out a bitter laugh as I watch him struggle, clawing at the ice, his body trembling from the cold, but he knows it's too late.

In the silence of the night, I can feel the weight of what I'm about to do. This isn't some hero's moment, some dramatic final showdown. No. This is just me taking care of business, finishing what should've been done the moment he laid his eyes on her.

I grab his head, dragging him by his hair, forcing him to look up at me. "Sorry, Marcus," I murmur, almost disappointed. "But I've got better things to do than watch you choke on your own fear."

With a swift motion, I shove his head under the water, feeling the life drain from him as he thrashes beneath my grip. His body bucks against mine, his last desperate attempts to escape, but it doesn't matter.

I hold him there, watching as his struggles grow weaker, as his body goes limp. It's over. I pull my knife from his hand, watching as the last breath he takes is swallowed by the cold depths. His form is carried away, his body lost to the unforgiving water.

As the last bubble escapes his mouth, I pull back, leaving him in the freezing darkness. Nature will take care of the rest for me. His body will be frozen within forty-five minutes, and sink to the bottom of the pond, lost and forgotten.

It's a death better than he deserves.

"Now, that's done," I mutter, wiping the blood from my blade in the snow. "I've got a doe to catch."

And with that, I walk off, leaving the frozen pond— and Marcus's frozen body—behind me.

Chapter Nine

Sloan

A holiday display appears like a mirage through the falling snow – a wonderland of twinkling lights and larger-than-life decorations spread through a wooded area off the main street. Giant candy canes line the walkway, their red and white stripes glowing against the night. Inflatable snowmen bob around in the wind, and off in the distance I can hear Christmas music drifting through the air like a dream.

My entire body is buzzing with anticipation, every nerve ending alive and singing. The first encounter with Alex has left me charged, feeling electric, like I've been struck by lightning and miraculously survived. My fingers tremble as I push long strands of my hair back from my face, and I can still feel the ghost of his touch on my skin.

Who are you really, Alex?

The thought spins through my mind as I slow my pace, mesmerized by the scene before me. It's like stepping into a children's storybook, all sugar and light and magic. For a moment, I forget why I'm running, and I forget everything except the way the colored lights reflect off the pristine white snow. But my body remembers – God, does it remember.

"Sloan."

His voice cuts through the night like a blade, sending chills down my spine. A sound escapes my throat – something between a gasp and a desperate whimper – before I can stop it. I whirl around, heart pounding, but I can't see him through the chaotic maze of decorations and trees. The shadows between the lights seem darker somehow, deeper, and I know he's out there, watching. *Waiting.*

I should be running away as fast as I can. I should be playing hard to get and focusing on beating his ass to the church.

Instead, heat pools low in my stomach, and my pulse races with something that feels dangerously close to desire. Because this isn't the Alex Adams who makes polite conversation at his father's church functions. This isn't the man who calculates every angle before making a move. This isn't the man who texts me once a day if I'm lucky and only lasts two or three minutes once his dick is inside me.

This is something else. Something wild. Something hungry.

And God help me, I want more.

Come get me, Alex.

The thought makes me grin as I dart between towering nutcrackers, their painted faces seeming to watch my every move. My heart is hammering against my ribs so hard I almost wonder if he can hear it. The music grows louder – "Winter Wonderland" playing from hidden speakers, creating a surreal soundtrack for this game. Snow crunches behind me, and I don't have to look to know he's following.

Each step sends a thrill through my body. There's something primal about being hunted like this, something that awakens parts of me I never knew existed. The cheery, hairdresser Sloan who worries about fitting into his world feels far away right now. In her place is someone feral, someone who wants to see just how far she can push him, just how much of his careful control she can strip away.

I round a corner and stop dead in my tracks. There, in a small clearing, stands a life-sized gingerbread house. It's a masterpiece of holiday decoration – strings of white lights outline every edge, making it glow like something from a fairy tale. Mechanical elves work at tiny benches along the front, their movements accompanied by the whir of hidden motors. Painted gingerbread people spin slowly on rotating platforms, their smiles somehow eerie in the mixed light.

My heart skips, then races. It's beautiful. It's creepy. It's *perfect*.

Hide. Run. Stay. Wait.

My thoughts war with each other as adrenaline courses through my veins. The Alex I knew yesterday would never follow me here. That Alex worried about propriety, about appearances, about what people would think. But *this* Alex? The one who's been hunting me through the snow? I have no idea what he's capable of, and the thought makes me shiver with anticipation.

Before I can think better of it, I duck inside, closing the door as I enter. The interior is smaller than I expected, more of a shed than a house, but the decorations continue here. Lights strung along the ceiling cast everything in a warm glow, and the walls are painted to look like frosted gingerbread, complete with candy decorations. The music is clearer here – "Silent Night" now, the soft melody at odds with the way my pulse is racing.

me shatters at the raw hunger in those two words. Gone is the polished pronunciation his mother spent years perfecting. Gone is the careful restraint he usually wears like armor.

This voice belongs to a predator. And I am gloriously, *willingly* caught.

Outside, the mechanical elves continue their endless work. Inside, time seems to stop as Alex's hand tangles in my hair, tilting my face up to his. The contrast between the innocent holiday cheer surrounding us and the heat in his eyes makes me feel a euphoric high. My entire world narrows to this moment, to his touch, to the way he's looking at me like he wants to consume me whole.

"Alex," I whisper, but he silences me with a thumb stroke down my bottom lip that steals my breath. I've seen that look before. It's a look that promises pleasure and pain, and fuck me, I *want* it all.

"Open," he commands, leaving no room for argument in his tone.

I do as he says, parting my lips while he unzips his pants, making quick work of freeing his cock from the tight confinements of his pants. He's rock hard as soon as he springs free, and my eyes go wide at the delicious sight. He's so much *bigger* than I remember. Then again, maybe that's because I've never seen him quite this hard before.

My mouth waters as I take him in, and I run my tongue across my bottom lip. He lets out a low, barely audible growl of approval when he sees how eager I am for him.

"You're going to suck my cock so hard we'll both be seeing stars," he tells me. "You're going to let me fuck your face until you think you're going to pass out, and then you'll let me keep going."

I nod, looking up at him through doe eyes. I suddenly understand why he's been calling me that. *His sweet doe.* I'm a deer fleeing from her vicious predator. But I want this one to catch me. To fuck me and to have his way with me. Tonight, I'm *his* to play with.

"Good girl," he praises my nod.

Tilting my head back, Alex grips his cock, bouncing it on my soft lips a few times before pressing against them, pushing his way into my mouth. I open for him without hesitation, letting him slide into me as far as he wants to go. He's slow and shallow at first, taking his time to let me tongue coat his cock in saliva. I groan against him when he thrusts his hips into my face, pressing himself deeper down my throat. I almost gag on him, but I grip his thighs to maintain control. It's too early to lose control.

Alex's head falls back as he gets lost in the tightness of my throat, and it quickens his pace. Both hands wrapped through my hair, he fucks my face in a steady rhythm for several strokes before he slams himself to the back of my throat, completely cutting off my airway. My eyes go wide when I can't breathe, and when I pull back, he holds my head steady in place.

"Take it like you're supposed to," he warns, reminding me that *he* is the one in control right now.

Alex removes one hand from my hair to reach for a string of lights hanging above us, and he yanks it down. He pulls his cock from my mouth to wrap the cord around my neck, making me wear it like a choker.

"Mmm," he purrs. "Much better."

I bite my bottom lip as I look up at him, giving him the sexiest look I can manage while he's cutting off my airway with the string of lights.

Alex's cock is back at my lips in an instant, and this time he doesn't hesitate to force his way into my mouth. I reach for my clit to pleasure myself while he uses my face, and I cry out around his cock as soon as my fingers find that swollen spot. It encourages him to keep going, to fuck my face harder and faster. I can't breathe at all, and part of me is scared he won't know when to stop and he'll keep going until I pass out. But I have to keep going. I won't fight him. He caught me twice fair and square, and now he gets to bask in his reward. The truth is, I'm fucking loving this and my pussy is sopping wet for him as he uses me to pleasure himself.

I continue moaning around his cock, sending vibrations through him. His hips buck as he nears his climax, and I swirl my fingers over my clit faster in response. I want us to come together.

Pulling on the lights harder, he uses them as reigns to control my upper body. I'm completely and utterly at his mercy right now. My stomach tightens as his dick swells in my mouth. He's on the verge of cumming.

My orgasm begins when he makes the most primal, unhinged sound. He's practically roaring as he comes, using my throat to milk himself dry and force me to take every last drop of him. I make myself come with him, and stars form in the corners of my vision as I near the point of blacking out. He's pushing me dangerously close to losing consciousness. I don't know how much longer I can hold on.

"Such a good fucking girl," he grunts, emptying the last bit of himself down my throat.

Right as my orgasm fades he lets go of the light, releasing me from his grasp and freeing his cock from my mouth. I fall back, gasping for air. Tears are running down both sides of my face and my lipstick is definitely smudged down my chin. But I don't fucking care. The look in his dark eyes tells me he doesn't care either. He's eating this shit up.

We're both breathing hard. The lights cast shadows across his masked face, making him look almost savage. Beautiful and dangerous, like a wolf. His thumb traces my lower lip, and I can feel the tremors running through his body, the way he's barely holding himself in check.

"Run," he says, his voice low and still rough with lust. "One hour left, my sweet doe. Make it count."

I stare at him, trying to catch my breath, trying to process everything that he just did. The music has changed again – "Let It Snow" now. My whole body feels like a live wire, every nerve ending screaming, *pleading* for more.

"Run," he repeats, and this time there's an edge to his voice that makes me shiver. "Or I'll catch you again, and you know what happens when I catch you for a third time..."

The promise in those words gets me moving. I scramble to my feet, adjusting my dress with shaking hands. My reflection in the window shows hair messed beyond repair, lips swollen, cheeks flushed. I look thoroughly ravished, and the sight sends another wave of heat through me. This is what Alex Adams can do when he lets go. *This* is what happens when the perfect facade cracks.

I pause at the door, looking back at him. He's still watching me with those predator's eyes, his usual perfect composure nowhere to be seen.

"What if I want you to catch me?" I tease, surprised by the huskiness in my own voice. In this moment, I don't care about his family's expectations or society's rules. I want more of *this* – more of him, raw and unrestrained.

He's silent for a moment while he watches me, making my heart thump harder. When he finally speaks again, his voice is so feral it scares me. He no longer sounds like himself. "Then run faster."

I burst out of the gingerbread house and back into the snowy night. The mechanical elves watch my escape with their painted eyes, still moving in their never ending dance. The music fades as I get farther and farther away.

One hour left. One hour to make it to the church. One hour before he does… what? The uncertainty thrills me almost as much as the chase itself.

Behind me, I hear the gingerbread house door open again, and my pulse spikes. Every cell in my body screams to turn around, to let him catch me again, to discover what other darkness he's been hiding. But I force myself forward, running through the wonderland of lights and snow.

The hunt is on.

And this time, I'm not sure if I'm running away or running toward something. All I know is that I'm running, and somewhere in this snowy night, Alex is following.

The colored lights blur around me as I pick up speed, freshly fallen snow crunching beneath my boots. My scalp tingles where he gripped my hair. Ahead lies the unknown – more challenges, more chase, more of whatever the fuck this game is that we're playing. Behind me lies the gingerbread house with its mechanical decorations and its secrets, and somewhere in between is Alex, hunting me through this winter wonderland of a town.

One hour left to run. One hour left to play. One hour left to discover just how deep his hunger for me goes.

I run faster, grinning into the snowy night as snow blasts my face, my whole body alive.

I'm ready for it all. Ready to see just how far Alex will go when he finally lets himself fall.

The night stretches ahead of me, full of promise and danger and desire.

And I run toward it, laughing like a fucking maniac.

Chapter Ten

Asher

She still thinks I'm Alex.

The thought lingers in my mind like the fading echo of her laugh, a secret so delicious it's almost better than the game itself. *Almost.* My cock is still hard, pulsing with the memory of her soft lips, the way she gagged and fought to breathe, and yet didn't pull away.

She didn't stop. *God*, she didn't stop.

My body hums with cocky satisfaction. Twice now, I've caught her, and both times she's crumbled so beautifully under me.

But the third time… Oh, the third time is when I'll truly make her mine.

I move silently through the snow, my steps muffled by its fresh, powdery layer. Sloan's ahead, darting between glowing decorations and weaving through the trees. Her silhouette flashes in and out of view, framed by the goddamn kaleidoscope of holiday lights. She's breathtaking, her wild and untamed energy feeding the predator in me, the part that's always craved something more raw and real than the polished life my family always demanded of me.

She's running fast, her hair a messy tangle around her flushed face. She knows exactly what she's doing—how she's taunting me. My sweet doe knows just how to be the perfect fucking prey. The way she glances back every so often, the grin on her swollen lips when she spots me—she wants this as much as I do, even if she doesn't fully understand what she's inviting in.

"Run, sweet doe," I murmur, my voice dark and slow, dripping with anticipation. "The longer you flee, the sweeter the catch will be. And once I have you, you won't escape again." My tone is low, laced with a promise, a thrill that hums through the words, a mix of lust and dominance. It's a predator's patience, savoring every second of the hunt, knowing the moment I close in, she'll be mine.

You're so fucking perfect, Sloan. And you think I'm him.

It's almost cruel, really, how easy it's been to step into Alex's shoes tonight. All it took was the ski mask and a little mimicry of his tone to get her running. He would have never understood her the way I do. His entire life he's been too busy playing the golden boy, the perfect obedient son.

Ahead, the music swells, leading me to the heart of the town's holiday festival. A nativity scene is set up in the town square, surrounded by a crowd that sways in time with the carolers' voices. The scene is almost idyllic—if not for the sharp edge of my desire slicing through the air.

I spot Sloan at the edge of the gathering, her movements frantic yet calculated. She's looking for an escape route, but she doesn't want to make it too easy. She's not just running away; she's daring me to catch her.

Challenge fucking accepted.

I duck into the crowd, moving through clusters of people with ease. My height gives me an advantage, allowing me to see her as she pushes past a group of children clustered around a hot chocolate stand. Her head swivels, her eyes scanning the dense crowd of people in search of me, and for a moment, I let her think she's lost me.

Her relief is short-lived.

In one swift motion, I step into her line of sight, just long enough for her to see me, then disappear again into the crowd. Her gasp is audible even over the choir's rendition of *O Holy Night.* The chase is on again, and my blood surges at the thrill of it. I'm not just hunting her.

I'm fucking with her. Toying with her. And my sweet doe, she fucking loves it.

She moves faster, her boots slipping slightly on the icy cobblestones as she weaves through the crowd. I follow at a measured pace, keeping to the shadows and savoring the way her body reacts to my presence—the quick glances over her shoulder, the way she clutches the hem of her dress, the flush spreading down her neck.

The sight of her running has my cock twitching with anticipation, aching to catch her one last time and bury myself so deep inside her that even heaven will hear her scream my name.

I step out of the crowd, keeping a safe distance but never letting her out of my sight. She reaches the edge of the square and pauses, looking toward the road that leads to the church. Her goal is clear, but the path there isn't. She's smart enough to know I'm anticipating her moves, and I can almost see the wheels turning in her mind as she debates her next step.

I grin under the mask and slip into the mob, disappearing for a moment. Her head whips around, searching for me, and the thrill of her rising panic sends a jolt of satisfaction through me.

God, she's beautiful like this—alive, flushed, and desperate.

She pushes past a cluster of people gathered near a life-size camel prop, her shoulders tight and determined. Her breath mists in the air, and I watch as she briefly stops to adjust her dress, brushing snow off the hem. A mistake. She's wasting time, and I make my move, slipping closer.

But before I can get too near, she spots me—or at least she thinks she does. Her lips curl into a grin, and she darts away, running faster toward the edge of town where the lights thin, and the trees start to thicken.

Good. She's heading for the tree farm.

The tree farm is perfect. Dark, winding paths, and enough cover for me to stay hidden until *I* decide to reveal myself again. Her energy is waning; I can see it in the way she staggers slightly in her step as she dodges around another towering display of reindeer. She's been running hard, playing this game with everything she has, like the perfect little playmate.

And I admire her for it. She's never intended to make this easy, and I wouldn't want her to.

The fight is half the fucking fun.

I pick up my pace, moving down a side street that cuts through the edge of the park. It's quieter here, the music and chatter of the crowd fading into the distance. Snow falls heavier now, blanketing everything in soft white, muffling my steps.

The tree farm is just ahead, its entrance marked by a glowing arch of colored lights. Rows upon rows of evergreens stretch into the darkness, their shapes looming like silent sentinels. It's the kind of place that swallows sound, where shadows linger and light struggles to reach.

I slip through the arch, anticipation coiling tight in my chest.

She's not far. I can feel it.

I move between the trees, staying close to the trunks, watching for movement. The snow has started to fall in thicker sheets, making visibility harder. Not that it matters. I know this place like the back of my hand.

A branch cracks somewhere up ahead, and my grin widens. She's trying to be quiet, but she doesn't know these paths the way I do. I pick up my pace, slipping through the rows of trees like a shadow.

She's still running, and I can hear her labored breaths now, the sound cutting through the stillness.

This is it. The third catch.

Chapter Eleven
Sloan

My lungs burn with each breath of frosted air, and my legs shake with exhaustion, but I've never felt more alive. The tree farm materializes out of the darkness like something from a fever dream – endless rows of evergreens standing tall in the moonlight. Snow blankets everything, pristine and untouched, reflecting the silvery light until it seems the whole farm is a mirage of diamonds and shadows. The church lies somewhere beyond the silent forest, and with it, either my victory or my sweet surrender.

Pulling my phone from my pocket, I check the time.

Thirty minutes until midnight.

Half an hour until this game ends – assuming I win it. There's no telling how long Alex will keep me in the church if he wins. Afterall, nothing is off-limits if he catches me again. He's faster than I am, so I have no doubt he'll be able to beat me to the church if he catches me for the third time.

My boots sink deeper into the snow with each step, making my thighs scream in protest. But it's nothing compared to the other aches in my body – the delicious soreness that reminds me of Alex's touch, of the way he's shattered every preconception I had about him tonight. My scalp still burns where he held my hair, a stark contrast to the biting cold of the winter air.

Who knew he had such a dark side?

The thought of him sends liquid heat through my veins despite the freezing temperature. No more than a few hours ago, I thought I knew Alex Adams. Thought I *understood* the careful way he moved through the world, all straight lines and sharp edges, just like his father.

Now... God, now I'm not sure I ever knew him at all.

I weave between the trees, trying to make my path as unpredictable as possible while fighting against snow that reaches halfway up my legs. Each step is a battle – lift, push, sink, recover. The cold penetrated my boots hours ago, turning my feet into blocks of ice, but the rest of me burns for his touch. For his transformation. For the way proper, controlled Alex became something animalistic and hungry in the darkness.

My breath comes in frosty puffs as I push forward, each exhale a cloud of crystallized desperation. The silence is deafening – the kind of quiet that only exists in snowfall, where the whole world seems to stop. I can't hear anyone following me, can't see any signs of pursuit, but that means nothing. I've learned that lesson twice tonight already.

The memory of the gingerbread house with its mechanical elves and twinkling lights sends another wave of heat coursing through my frozen body. The way he looked at me there, like something primal had finally broken free of its chains. The sounds he made... God, I never thought I'd hear sounds like that from a man who follows God so closely.

Focus, Sloan. Get to the fucking church. Win the goddamn game.

But do I want to win? The question hits me as I pause behind a particularly large pine, leaning against its thick branches to catch my breath. My heartbeat thunders in my ears, equal parts exertion and anticipation. The church means the end of the game. The end of this wild, kinky version of Alex who seems to find me no matter where I hide. The end of discovering just how deep his darkness goes.

Unless I lose. Unless I surrender to him, and then… maybe this is only the beginning.

How am I supposed to celebrate Christmas with his family after this? How can I sit across from him at his mom's dining table, making polite conversation about the weather, when I know what lurks beneath his perfect manners? When all I'll want to do is lay across the table and let him have his way with me.

The silence wraps around me as I rest against the tree. Every muscle in my body trembles with fatigue, but beneath the exhaustion is anticipation. The moonlight peeking through the clouds creates strange shadows between the trees, making every dark space look like it might be hiding him. The thought should be enough to get my legs moving again. Instead, it makes my pulse quicken, makes heat gather between my thighs despite the bone-deep cold.

I scan the darkness behind me, seeing nothing but endless rows of evergreens and undisturbed snow. The only footprints are my own, which are already being covered by the falling snowflakes. No movement. No sign of the predator I know is out there somewhere. The Alex I knew yesterday would never trudge through snow this deep in his expensive shoes. But *this* Alex? The one who's been hunting me through the night? I'm starting to think there's nothing he wouldn't do.

When I turn back around, he's there.

My heart stops, then explodes into a frantic rhythm as I stare into eyes that barely look human anymore. He's breathing hard, his perfect posture gone, snow dusting his shoulders. His eyes make my knees weak as I stare at him through the black ski mask.

Every cell in my body is screaming *yes*.

"Alex," I breathe, but that's all I manage before he moves. One moment I'm standing alone, the next I'm pinned against the tree trunk, its bark rough against my back even through my overcoat. His body cages mine, radiating heat that makes the winter air between us disappear entirely. The contrast is dizzying – ice at my back, fire at my front.

"Now I get to fuck you," he growls, and God, his *voice*. When did proper, controlled Alex start sounding like that? Like he's barely holding onto his humanity? Like he's two seconds away from burning the world for me?

Alex's cock presses against me through his pants, and I let out a breathless gasp, my hands clutching at his shoulders through the layers of his coat. The intensity in his gaze sends shivers down my spine, forcing a moan to slip through my lips. My eyes flutter at the feel of the rough fabric of his ski mask against my skin when he leans in closer, his lips so close to mine yet unable to touch.

Desire rips through me, igniting every nerve ending in my body as I arch into him, begging for more. His hands roam over my body, firm fingers tracing my curves through my red sweater dress. My torn black tights leave my pussy exposed to the cold air, making me need him that much more.

Without words and without hesitation, Alex hikes my dress up over my hips, exposing my bare pussy even more. The cold air bites down on my skin, making me cry out.

"I need you," I whimper, gripping him tighter. "I need you to fuck me right now."

Alex doesn't make me wait. He unfastens his pants, freeing his cock. My mouth waters as he strokes himself a few times. It's so cold, but he's so fucking hard for me.

Lining himself up with my entrance, he rubs the head of his cock over my clit and through my slick folds several times before pushing his way into me. My head falls back with delight as he slides inside of me, filling me so fully that I think I might burst.

"Oh fuck," I cry out. "You're so fucking big."

Alex slams into me harder, making me take every delicious inch of him. He grunts against my neck as he leans into me, pounding me into the tree. We're shaking the tree so violently that the snow is falling from the branches, covering our shoulders in white. But I don't care. All I can think about is how fucking good his cock feels inside of me. And how much I fucking love this side of Alex. I'll gladly get on my knees for him every day for the rest of my life if he feeds me cock this good. I'll never tire of the way he thrusts inside of me, stretching me fuller than I thought I could take.

I meet his strokes, pushing off the tree each time he buries himself inside of me. He feels fucking perfect. Like his cock was made to fill my pussy perfectly.

Groaning, Alex pulls his head back from where he had it buried in my neck, and he fists his fingers through my hair, forcing me to watch him as he fucks me. I meet his intense stare, watching them through his ski mask. My lips part, my jaw dropping when I see flecks of gold in Alex's normally brown eyes. They're almost glowing against the moonlight, and suddenly I don't feel like I'm staring at Alex.

It's like he notices my hesitation, and he breaks our stare, spinning me around to face the tree trunk so that he can fuck me from behind. My mind immediately wanders away from the change in his eyes, getting lost in the feeling of his cock slamming into me again.

I grip the tree trunk, letting the bark scrape against my fingers. Alex's hands are on both sides of my hips, and he's using his hold to thrust me into him harder. My ass bounces off of him with each stroke, and soon we're making a loud clapping sound that breaks the dead silence of the tree farm.

Snow and sex. The only two things filling the air.

"Fuck," I moan, using what little strength I have left to hold myself up against the tree.

"Take it," he growls, pushing into me harder. "Fucking take it."

And I do. The walls of my pussy clench around his cock, baring down as an orgasm hits me out of nowhere. Alex roars against the night, spilling himself inside of me so furiously I come twice, back to back waves of pleasure that steamroll their way through my body.

Alex steps back after his last stroke, letting his cock fall. He slaps my ass so hard it makes me yelp and arch my back, which makes my pussy involuntarily clench, missing the fullness of his dick. Tucking himself back inside his pants, he helps me pull my dress back down and secures my overcoat around my body to trap my body heat inside of it.

When he finally steps back, we're both gasping. Snow continues to fall, silent and steady, already covering our footprints. His eyes are still wild, pupils blown wide, and I realize with a start that I love this version of him. Love the way he's completely unleashed, totally present.

"Ten minutes," he says without having to check the time, his voice rough like gravel. "Get to the church before me or you're mine."

The words send electricity down my spine. Aren't I already? Haven't I already lost the game entirely? There's not a chance in the world I'm going to beat him to the church. All I can do now is prepare myself for what happens when I arrive there. For what happens when I surrender to him and give myself to him entirely in the one place I never expected to.

"Run," he commands, stepping back, and the sudden loss of his heat makes me shiver violently. "Run, Sloan. This is your last chance before there's no turning back."

My legs feel like jelly as I push away from the tree. Every muscle protests – too much running, too much tension, too much pleasure. The cold air hits my heated skin like a slap, making me inhale sharply.

I force myself forward through the deep snow, each step an uphill battle against exhaustion and gravity. Behind me, I hear nothing – but in reality, that means nothing. I've learned tonight that Alex can move like a ghost when he wants to, appearing and disappearing like a fucking shadow.

The moonlight breaks through the clouds above the trees, casting enough light to find my way. My breath comes in sharp pants. Less than ten minutes to make it through this silent forest of Christmas trees, to find the church, and to win this game. I can't give up now. Not when I'm so close to the church.

But my mind keeps dragging me back to the tree, to his touch, to the way he growled my name like it was something both sacred and profane all at once. Each memory of his cock thrusting inside me makes it harder to run, harder to focus on anything except how wet I am.

Focus, I think, shaking my head at myself. It's fucking pathetic how worked up I am right now. I'm like a bitch in heat who can only focus on one thing: dick.

But God, I don't want this night to end. I don't want to go back to the way things were before today. Not to the stale-by-comparison Alex who doesn't let this darkness so much as peek through the cracks of his facade.

The snow is falling faster now, thick flakes catching in my eyelashes, making the world blur at the edges. Or maybe that's just exhaustion. Maybe that's just desire. Maybe that's just what happens when you've been thoroughly claimed by someone you thought you knew, only to discover you never really knew them at all.

I stumble in the snow, but I catch myself and quickly recover, forcing myself to keep moving. My legs are trembling with fatigue, but I can't stop now.

Part of me wants to fall. *Wants* to let him beat me to the church. *Wants* to discover what he's been saving for the end of this game.

Through the trees ahead, I catch a glimpse of something – a spire, maybe, dark against the night sky. The church? Hope and disappointment war in my chest as I collapse in the snow, unable to take another step. Pulling out my phone, I check the time. *11:59 pm.*

Fuck. One minute. I won't make it.

Alex is probably already there. Watching. *Waiting.*

I'm not even mad. Just exhausted and cold.

Chapter Twelve

Asher

I should've been more careful.

That's my first thought when I hear the crunch of boots on snow behind me. It's a reminder that I'm not as invincible as I think. But then again, *careful* isn't fun, is it? If I was careful, I wouldn't have the rush I get from this—getting to play the game. Committing the sins my parents always expected of me, watching people crumble. That's the kind of high I live for now.

The second thought? If he's stupid enough to follow, he deserves what's coming. Loose ends aren't messy—they're a chance to tie up everything in a neat, bloody bow. There's always someone lurking around, thinking they can stop the inevitable.

But when it comes to me, they're never right.

The sound of frantic footsteps catches up to me. His breath comes in short, sharp bursts, puffing out in the cold night air. His footsteps echo, panicked, like they know they're getting closer to their own demise.

I stop mid-step, letting him see my silhouette framed by the moonlight. The stillness is intentional. I want him to think he's caught me off guard, that he has some kind of control over this situation. That's how it always starts—the false sense of confidence before everything goes to shit.

I expect nothing less from this piece of shit.

He freezes for a moment, then tries to step back. Fucker is probably hoping he can turn around and run, but he's too slow. Too predictable. Rats always run forward, even when they know the trap is waiting.

"What's the matter?" I call over my shoulder, my voice light and playful, deliberately soft. "You lost, friend?"

I don't need to look at him to know his eyes are wide with fear, his breath shallow. It's exactly what I want to hear. The *desperation*.

"You're sick, man!" His voice shakes, but there's anger in it, a spark of self-righteousness that grates on my nerves. "You're damn well deserving of rotting in the deepest pits of hell."

I turn slowly, the crunch of snow beneath my boots echoing in the cold night air. The moonlight glints off his face, casting shadows that make his wide, terrified eyes seem almost unreal. His breath comes in sharp, shallow bursts, and I can see the fear dripping off him like sweat, freezing before it hits the ground. He's trembling, but there's a defiance in him—one that makes me smile.

I take a step closer, my voice low and deliberate. "Burn in hell, huh?" I chuckle darkly, letting the words hang between us. "You're upset because you think you have the power to damn me. But what you don't realize is… hell's a place for those who lose control. And I, my friend, have never been more in control than I am right now."

His jaw tightens. His fists clench at his sides, knuckles turning white. I can see the muscles in his neck straining under the weight of his rage. It's pathetic.

"I saw you," he snarls, his voice raw with accusation. "You fucking killed Marcus. You drowned him, held him under the water like it was nothing!"

I grin. A slow, wicked curve of my lips. "Because it was."

The words hit him like a slap, his expression twisting in a way that's both horrifying and… satisfying. There it

129

is—fear, disbelief, and disgust all rolled into one. "You're insane!" he spits, his voice cracking under the weight of what he's just realized.

"No," I say, tilting my head again, letting the edge of my smile widen. "Just thorough."

I take a step forward, and his eyes bulge. His chest heaves. He knows what comes next. He knows this is the end of the line. But it doesn't matter. None of it matters.

He stumbles back, but I don't let him go far. I close the distance between us, fast and decisive.

"I'm going to the cops," he snaps, his voice trembling, a mix of fear and defiance leaking through. "You're done. You think you can do this and just walk away?"

I let out a laugh, cold and sharp, like glass breaking. "Walk away? Buddy, I'm planning a whole parade. But go ahead. Tell them Alex did it. See how far that gets you."

He pulls out his phone, fingers shaking as he starts recording, the screen lighting up with his shaky image. "I'm going to make sure they know everything," he says, his voice filled with a desperate hope.

The look on his face is almost pathetic as he thinks that's his salvation.

I step closer, a slow grin curling at the corner of my mouth. "You think that's going to save you?" I ask, my voice dripping with amusement.

His confusion deepens, his brow furrowing as he stares at the screen, trying to make sense of the situation. But he doesn't realize what I know—that at this hour, in this darkness, there's no way anyone will be able to tell me apart from my brother.

I move closer, the shadows swallowing me, and lean in just close enough for him to hear my next words, my tone as smooth as silk but carrying a dangerous edge.

"You should've thought this through a little more," I whisper, my smile widening as I slowly pull the ski mask over my head, revealing my face to him in the dim light. "You're recording a ghost."

"Alex?" He mutters the name like it's a whisper, like a prayer.

There it is.

I can see the exact moment the pieces click together in his mind. His eyes widen, darting over my face, my frame.

"You... Holy shit, you're—"

It feels so damn good to finally reveal myself. To let him see me for who I really am, even though he has no idea

I'm not my twin. I can see the realization dawn in his eyes, the betrayal running deep.

"Alex," I finish for him, my voice mocking the reverence he's clearly trying to show. "That's right. The golden boy, the good son, the saint of Holly Grove." I laugh. It's not a joyful sound. "Bet you didn't know I had it in me, huh?"

He looks as if he's about to argue, but the crack in his voice gives him away.

"It can't be," he says, but there's no conviction in it anymore. He's grasping at straws.

"Oh, no. It's true," I say, my voice laced with venom. "I, Alex fucking Adams killed Marcus. I snapped. Poor fucking me, finally breaking under all the pressure and weight of always being so goddamn perfect."

He shakes his head, like he's trying to make sense of everything I'm saying. It's almost pathetic. He takes another step back, stumbling.

"No, no, this—this doesn't make sense. Alex wouldn't do this. He's... He's not like *you*."

I can't help but laugh. It's sharp, loud, and echoes off the trees. I step forward, closing the gap. My breath mixes with the cold night air, a cloud of steam coming from my mouth as I lean in close, just inches from his ear.

"That's the best part, isn't it?" I whisper, the words cutting through the space between us like a knife. "Nobody would ever think it was me." I lean in closer. "Except it was."

His mouth opens, and a choked gasp escapes him, but no words follow. The silence is deafening.

"You're fucking lying," he says again, but the panic in his voice gives him away. He knows the truth now, even if he doesn't want to admit it.

I snap. I can feel it building inside of me, the anger, the thrill of the chase, the power. I let him lunge at me, but I'm ready for it. I let him land one solid punch, the pain blooming across my cheek in a way that only makes me smile wider. I lick the blood from my lip, savoring the taste of it.

"Nice," I say, cracking my neck, my hands loosening and tightening with anticipation. "My turn."

I drive my fist into his gut, hard and fast. The air leaves his lungs in a violent gasp, his body jerking from the impact. He stumbles backward but doesn't fall. I don't let him. I grab the collar of his jacket, yanking him close, my nose brushing against his ear.

"For thine is the kingdom," I whisper, a mockery of reverence. The words spill from me like a fucking chant.

I slam my forehead into his face. The sound of crunching cartilage fills the air, and he screams. Blood pours down his face like a waterfall, hot and sticky.

"Forever and ever, amen," I whisper, pulling the knife from my belt. I don't need to look at it. The feel of the cold steel in my hand is enough.

The fight is over. He's over.

I straddle him, pinning him down to the snowy ground with one knee, pressing my weight onto his chest. He thrashes beneath me, hands grasping at my arm, but he's weak, his movements slow and desperate.

The knife rises and then falls.

With each strike, the blade sinks deeper and quicker. His screams dissolve into wet gurgles as blood pours from his wounds, coating the snow around us. My movements are precise, measured, each cut satisfying in its brutality.

Fuck, this feels good.

When I finally stop, my arms ache, my chest is heaving, and the snow around us is painted a deep crimson color. He twitches once, his body spasming, and then goes still. I sit back, panting, as I let the weight of what just happened settle over me. The cold air feels sharp in my lungs, but it doesn't touch the fire burning in my chest.

I glance down at his face. It's not just fear anymore. It's betrayal. There's no mistaking it. He thought he stood a chance. Thought he could stop me from ending his pathetic life.

Pathetic.

I grin as a sudden rustling draws my attention, the sound sharp in the still night. My head snaps toward it, and I spot a squirrel darting up the trunk of a tree, its tail flicking nervously. Curious, I approach the base of the tree and pause, my gaze falling on something unexpected—a saw, propped haphazardly against the trunk.

The teeth of the blade gleam faintly in the moonlight, the edges worn but sharp enough to do the job. No doubt, it was left behind by one of the families who came here today, eager to chop down their perfect Christmas tree.

Hell yes.

A slow, deliberate smile stretches across my face as an idea takes root. This is too perfect. The kind of opportunity you can't plan for but that makes the whole thing sweeter. I wrap my hand around the saw's handle, the rough wood cool beneath my palm, and lift it.

The thought of what's to come sets my pulse racing. The art of this isn't just in the blood—it's in the precision, the creativity. And now, I have the perfect tool to elevate the moment.

I start sawing through his wrist, each pass of the blade slicing through flesh and tendon with a satisfying crunch. The wetness of his blood, thick and warm, coats my hands as I work. His body twitches again, the last remnants of life flickering out of him, but this fucker is far beyond saving now. No amount of pleading or remorse can bring him back from the edge he's pushed himself to.

When I finally sever the hand from the wrist, I hold it up to the light. The severed hand dangles loosely from my grip, fingers splayed out like a grotesque offering to dear old daddy's precious God who's watching.

The hand is the perfect fucking gift.

It's exactly what I needed.

"Thanks for the gift, dude," I murmur, my voice low and dripping with satisfaction as I lift the severed hand higher, tilting it just so the moonlight catches the pale skin and crimson edges. It's almost poetic, in a twisted, macabre way—a testament to what I've become, what I've always been.

This is it. The perfect offering, the ultimate declaration. Sloan, my sweet, naïve doe, will know exactly who it is from the moment she opens it. No more shadows. No more playing the "good son". No more hiding behind a mask. After tonight, she'll see me—really see me—for who I am.

And she'll accept me. How could she not? After all, she's been part of this game from the start. Every step, every move, every choice she made led her to this moment. To me.

The thought of her unwrapping the box sends a thrill through me. I can already picture her face—the way her eyes will widen, not in fear, but in understanding. She'll finally see the truth. She'll understand the lengths I've gone to for her, the sacrifices I've made. This is love, raw and unfiltered, stripped of pretense.

I chuckle, low and dark, running my thumb over the cold, lifeless fingers. "No more secrets, Sloan," I whisper, almost to myself. "After tonight, there's nothing to hide. You'll know me—every piece of me. And you'll love me for it."

I stand, brushing the snow from my knees, and take a moment to admire the scene before me. The blood, dark and rich, already soaks into the ground, its crimson hue staining the pristine white snow like a grotesque work of art. The body lies there, lifeless and discarded, as though it had never mattered in the first place. Everything is exactly as it fucking should be.

But I'm not one to leave loose ends.

I bend down, grabbing the poor fuck's phone with the video of *Alex*, ending the recording before tucking it into my pocket. I pull Alex's phone from my other pocket, and toss it to the crimson snow next to the body. After all, I have no use for it anymore and if the video evidence isn't enough, finding my pathetic twin's phone on the dead guy's body pretty much seals his conviction. Especially with him being MIA. People will just assume he ran. Took off to avoid a murder charge on top of his ungodly sins.

I reach for a nearby branch and sweep it across the blood-slicked snow, masking the worst of the carnage. Then, methodically, I start shoveling handfuls of fresh snow over the body, the icy cold numbing my fingers as I work. The snow piles up quickly, burying the lifeless form in a pristine white shroud. Layer by layer, I erase the evidence, entombing him beneath the wintry blanket until the ground looks undisturbed once more.

I step back, surveying my work. The scene now looks untouched, peaceful even with the freshly fallen snow.

Perfectly hidden, perfectly forgotten. Just like he deserves.

But there's one last thing to do.

I glance toward the trail, knowing the gift shop isn't far. My pulse quickens as I move, feet crunching against the snow with hurried steps. The cold bites at my face as I tuck the severed hands into my pockets, but I barely notice, too focused on getting this shit done and getting to the church.

When I reach it, the contrast is almost laughable. The gift shop glows warm and inviting, decked out with garlands and twinkling lights, as if mocking the horrors I just left a few steps away from their door. Inside, shelves are lined with bright ribbons, holiday trinkets, and neatly stacked boxes waiting to hold something special. Something unforgettable.

I tuck the ski mask into my back pocket before pushing open the door, the faint jingle of a bell breaking the eerie silence of the night. The air inside is warm and smells faintly of cinnamon. It's offensively cheerful, but perfect. Just the place to find what I need to make this gift as memorable as possible.

"Evening, Alex. We're just about to close," an old woman calls from behind the counter, her voice weary but polite.

"No problem," I reply smoothly, flashing a disarming smile. "I'll be quick." My tone is light, casual—

nothing to draw attention, nothing to linger in her mind after I'm gone.

Warm light spills from the fake holiday candles spread out around the store, casting a golden glow on the small space.

I head straight for the display of gift boxes, the red and green foil paper shining obnoxiously under the twinkling lights. My eye catches on a shelf containing dark, sleek boxes. *Perfect.* I grab the biggest one and pair it with a spool of thick black ribbon sitting on the counter nearby.

Dropping both items onto the counter, I offer the old woman another easy smile as I fish a few bills from my pocket.

"Just these," I say, sliding the money across.

She rings me up with a polite nod. "Merry Christmas, and say hi to your parents for me," she offers with a faint smile, her voice tired but genuine.

"Right, of course. You, too," I reply, my tone almost cheerful as I pick up the bag. "Have a great night."

As I leave the shop, the bell jingling behind me, I can't help but laugh. The thought of Sloan opening that box, her sweet doe eyes widening in horror when she sees the contents, is almost too much to bear. The image plays over and over in my mind, each time becoming more vivid, more real. She'll get it. She'll finally understand the lengths I'm willing to go to when it comes to protecting her, *us*.

I circle around to the side of the building, out of sight of any prying eyes. The cold bites at my skin, but it doesn't bother me. This is where the real work begins. I crouch down under the dim light of a single bulb, the glow casting long shadows against the brick wall.

The hand fits perfectly inside the box, the severed wrist pressing against the bottom like it was made for it. I press the lid down, feeling the cold, slick surface of the skin as I arrange it just right. Satisfied, I grab the wide black ribbon I just bought. It's shiny, it's sleek, and it's exactly what I need.

I wrap the ribbon around the box with meticulous care, tying it into a big, elaborate bow that's just a little too perfect. The end result is absurd, and that's exactly why it's so fitting. A festive façade for something far darker lurking inside.

Standing back, I admire my work under the moonlight. It's beautiful in its grotesque absurdity. A perfect little nightmare, wrapped in Christmas cheer. A gift no one could ever forget, no matter how much they might want to.

In just a few minutes, she'll learn that this was never Alex's fucking game. It's mine from the moment she opened that tiny black box.

When I reach the church, the back door creaks slightly as I push it open. The smell hits me first—wood polish and old books, with a faint undercurrent of stale cigar smoke.

My father's office hasn't changed. The same heavy oak desk, the same leather armchair. The same pictures lining the walls, all of them starring Alex.

Not a single one of me.

I clench my jaw, forcing myself to move on. None of that matters. Not anymore.

The church is silent, bathed in the golden glow of candlelight.

Just outside my father's office I hear the door creak open.

Sloan's here. She's late—two minutes.

Game over.

Chapter Thirteen

Sloan

The heavy wooden doors of the church creak open under my tired, trembling hands, and the sound echoes through the vast space like a death knell. 12:02 AM. Two minutes late. I've lost the game.

My legs nearly give out as I step inside, the sudden warmth making my frozen skin feel a thousand pin pricks. Every muscle screams from exhaustion – from running, from the cold, from what Alex has put my body through tonight. God, just thinking about it makes heat flood through my body, fighting against the bone-deep chill.

The church seems to breathe around me, old and knowing, filled with spirits. Moonlight filters through towering stained glass windows, casting jewel-toned shadows across worn marble floors. The air is thick with pine and perfume, lingering from midnight mass. I imagine all of the people sitting in the pews as I walk, and the wide variety of sins and secrets they hold close while listening to the service.

Our Father, who art in Heaven...

I almost laugh at the fragment of prayer that floats through my mind. Church was never my thing – too many rules, too much guilt, too little room for the messy reality of human desire. The Adams family, of course, have their own pew here, third row from the front, marked with a discrete brass plaque. I wonder what they would think if they knew what their perfect son has been doing tonight.

My wet boots echo on the tile as I make my way down the center aisle. Rows of empty pews stretch out on either side, their wood gleaming dully in the low light. Above, the vaulted ceiling disappears into darkness, but I can just make out the intricate carvings – angels and demons locked in eternal battle.

How appropriate.

The altar looms ahead, a masterpiece of carved stone and gold leaf, far too fancy for a town as small as this. A massive crucifix hangs above it, and even in the dim light, I can see the agony on Christ's face. The pain. The ecstasy.

A table of candles left lit makes shadows dance across the stations of the cross that line the walls. Each depicts its own form of suffering, its own blend of pain and transcendence. I've never understood the Catholic obsession with beautiful agony until tonight. Until Alex showed me how closely pleasure, pain, and exhaustion can dance together.

My legs are shaking so badly I have to lean against a pew. Every inch of my body aches — from the cold, from running, from *him*. The last encounter in the tree farm nearly broke me. It took everything I had to pull myself up from the snow, to force my frozen limbs to carry me the rest of the way here. Even knowing I'd lost, even knowing what that might mean.

Or maybe because of what that might mean.

The thought sends a shiver through me. Because the truth is, part of me slowed down on purpose. Part of me *wanted* to be late. *Wanted* to lose. *Wanted* to discover the grand finale Alex has been saving for the end of the night.

A door creaks behind me, the sound impossibly loud in the midnight silence. My heart leaps into my throat as footsteps echo off the floor — measured, unhurried. *Confident.* The walk of a predator who knows his prey is cornered.

I don't turn around. I can't. Every muscle in my body has locked up, caught between terror and anticipation.

"You're late." His voice slides down my spine like water dripping from an icicle. He's closer than I expected, just a few feet behind me. I can feel his presence like a physical weight, like gravity itself has shifted to pull me toward him.

"Two minutes," I whisper, and my voice sounds strange in the vast space, too breathy, too desperate. I turn to meet his gaze. "Only two minutes late."

"Late is late, Sloan." The ski mask should look ridiculous on him. Instead, it makes him look dangerous, predatory. A demon in disguise, here to claim what he's owed. "But I have to admit, you played the game... exceptionally well." The words roll off his tongue like silk.

He moves closer, and I grip the pew harder to keep from swaying toward him. Even after everything tonight – the chase, the catches, the countless moments of pleasure and pure exhaustion – my body still reacts to his presence like a moth to a flame. Like it knows something my mind is still trying to process.

"The game is over," he continues, and there's something in his voice I've never heard before. Something that makes my knees weak. "But rules are rules, and now nothing is off-limits."

The sound of something soft sliding against cardboard makes me turn to face him fully. In his gloved hands is a black box, elegant in its simplicity, wrapped with a black ribbon that seems to absorb what little light there is. My breath catches. After a night of so much suspense this small box somehow feels like the most dangerous thing yet.

"What is it?" The question escapes before I can stop it.

His laugh is low, husky. "Curious little thing, aren't you? But no. You don't get to know. Not yet." He steps closer, near enough that I can feel the heat radiating from his body, and can smell that distinctive mix of expensive cologne and primal male that's now him. "You don't get to open it until I'm done with you."

The words hang in the air between us, heavy with promise. Above us, the carved angels and demons seem to lean closer, as if they too want to know what comes next.

"And when will that be?" I manage to ask, proud that my voice only shakes slightly.

He reaches out, tracing one gloved finger down my cheek. Even through the leather, his touch burns, igniting my core. "When I've had my fill of you. When I've taken everything you have to give. When I've marked you so thoroughly that you'll never forget who you belong to."

The words should frighten me. Should make me run. Instead, they make me so wet I can feel the slickness between my legs without touching myself. His words make my breath catch in my throat. Because this isn't the Alex Adams who loyally follows mommy and daddy to the ends of the earth. This is something else. *Someone* else. Someone who's been hiding behind his perfect manners, waiting for the right moment – the right night – to break free.

"The game is over," he repeats, setting the black box carefully on the pew beside us. "But the night?" His hand slides into my hair, gripping hard enough to make me whimper out a small cry. "The night is just beginning."

I should feel sacrilegious, letting him touch me like this in a house of God. Should feel guilty about the way my body arches toward his, *hungry* for more despite my exhaustion. But all I feel is alive. Electrified. Like every moment before this was just preparation, just practice for this version of Alex.

His other hand comes up to trace my bottom lip, and even through the glove, I can feel him trembling slightly. Controlled Alex, proper Alex, *perfect* Alex – barely holding onto his composure. Because of me. Because of his game. Because of whatever's about to happen next.

The black box sits beside us, mysterious and promising. Could it be more cash? A few thousand dollars to spend on skimpy outfits? My mind wanders away from the box because right now, with Alex's hands on me and the suspense hanging in the air, it's the least interesting thing in the room.

"What are you going to do?" I ask, my bottom lip quivering with need between words.

Alex tsks, shaking his head. "It's not what I'm going to do, my sweet doe. It's what *you're* going to do."

"I don't have anything left to give," I admit, still leaning on the pew for support. "I don't know what you want me to do."

"I want you to ride me," he says immediately. "I want you to fuck my cock with that tight little cunt until you're too exhausted to move. And after that, I'll force your body to bounce on my cock until you're weeping for me to stop. I'll draw out every drop of pleasure your body holds until you're on the verge of passing out. You will give me all of you. You will give me *everything.*"

Alex grabs my chin between his fingers, forcing me to look at his dark eyes hiding behind the mask. They're hard, but those gold flecks are still there. How have I never noticed those before?

Pulling me from thought, he jerks me into the pews, forcing me down onto his lap so that I'm straddling him. His tone is sharp and possessive as he whispers against my ear. "Tell me you'll give me *everything*, Sloan. Tell me you're *mine*."

Trembling, I nod. "I'm yours."

His hands fall to my hips, and he's rubbing his thumbs over my sides. "Tell me you'll give me everything."

"I'll give you everything." My words are soft, barely audible.

Alex growls with approval, tightening his grip around my hips. "Take my cock out, and suck it before you fuck it with that perfect little pussy."

Without protest, I climb off his lap and lower myself to the floor, resting my weight on my knees. Alex plays with my long, tangled hair while I make quick work of unfastening his pants. I pull his already hardened dick from his pants, and then free it from his briefs. It's stiff in my hand, making my mouth water at both the sight and feel. Wetting my bottom lip with my tongue, I lean forward, opening until it's wide enough to fit him. His velvety cock slides into my mouth easily, and I let my tongue coat it in saliva the entire way in. I close my lips around him, moaning as I begin to bob up and down.

"Mmm," Alex moans when I take him all the way to the base of his cock. "Just like that."

I keep going, quickening my pace as I use my right hand to stroke his cock in unison with my head movements. My left hand is braced on the seat of the pew, and it's pretty much the only thing preventing me from falling over right now. My body is so far beyond the point of exhaustion, but I can't stop because who the fuck knows when Alex will act like this again? Who knows when I'll have the opportunity to give head and get fucked in an empty church on Christmas Eve night again?

I *need* this.

I *need* him.

Alex's hands lace through my hair, and he pushes down on the back of my head, forcing me to take him so far down my throat I can no longer breathe. He holds me there for a few seconds before yanking me back, leaving me gasping for air.

"Get on it," he demands, pointing toward his dick with his eyes.

I'm unsteady as I rise to my feet, and I have to use the back of the pew behind him as I climb back onto his lap, straddling his fully erect cock. Removing one hand from the pew, I grab him in my hand, lining up the head of his cock with my entrance. I'm already sopping wet, so he slides into me easily as I lower myself onto him. My pussy swallows him whole, taking him in one movement.

"Oh," I cry out in a moan, letting my head fall back as I begin bouncing up and down. Moving my hands to his shoulders, I use him for support while I ride him.

Alex pulls a knife out of nowhere, and I jump back when he brings it to my stomach.

"Don't stop," he barks, making me wince.

Slowly, I start moving again, watching his glistening blade closely with wide eyes. He pulls on the bottom of my dress, slipping the tip of the knife through it, and then he rips it up, cleanly slicing the fabric from my body. My boobs pop out, bouncing in his face while I keep the rhythm going.

"Fuck, yes," he hisses, setting the knife on the wood beside us and gripping my hips, slamming me down on his cock as hard as he can while taking one of my tits into his mouth. His tongue flicks out, lapping at my nipple and making it harden into a peak.

I cry out as the pleasure builds, radiating through my body. My legs are burning, but I push through because this is my chance to live out my most taboo fantasies. This is my "fuck you" to Alex's mom and dad.

This is my darkest desire come to life.

I bring my fingers to my clit, swirling over it so furiously that an orgasm crashes into me, making me bare down on his cock. I feel the heat of the liquid leaving me as I shatter internally, squirting for him. He leaves me no room to feel self-conscious about my body's sweet release when he bucks his hips beneath me, driving himself into me harder and forcing me to squirt harder.

Stars dance on the edges of my vision. Like sugar plum fairies performing a ballet just for us. Smiling, I put every last ounce of energy into pleasing Alex.

Tonight has been the best gift I could have ever asked for and more.

Merry fucking Christmas, Alex.

Chapter Fourteen
Asher

I watch her, every inch of her body moving on top of me, riding me like she's in a frenzy, lost in the moment. Her hips roll with a hunger I can't fucking ignore, pulling me closer to the edge as she moans, her head thrown back in pleasure. It's almost too much to handle—too fucking good. She's tight, her slick heat swallowing me, every movement sending shockwaves of raw pleasure coursing through me.

Her hands brace against my chest, her nails digging into my vest as she rides faster, pushing herself harder, taking me deeper with each roll of her hips. I can feel every inch of her, feel the way pussy pulses, clenches down around me, almost as if she's trying to hold me inside her. It's fucking intoxicating—like nothing else matters but this moment, this connection between us.

She feels it, too. My sweet doe is losing herself in it.

"God, you feel so fucking good," I mutter, my voice rough, low. My hands move to her hips, guiding her movements, pushing her down harder, making her take every inch of me hard and fast. "You like that? You like how deep I can go?"

Her breath quickens, her eyes squeezing shut as she rides me with more desperation. "Yes... yes, don't stop. Please..."

She's losing it. I know it's too much for her, but it's too fucking good. Her movements are wild now, erratic, and I'm right there with her, matching her rhythm, each thrust building the tension between us.

"You're perfect," I whisper against her skin through the cotton mask. "You're mine now, sweet doe. Every breath you take, every shiver that runs through you will remind you of who owns you. No more running. It's time to surrender. You hear me? *Mine.*"

She moans, the sound almost inaudible, but I catch it. The way she's getting lost in this, in me. She already came on my cock once, but when her body shudders, I know she's close again. I can feel it. Her walls are tightening around me, like she's trying to keep me inside her. She's desperate for it. I can't help but push harder, meeting her thrusts, driving deeper, taking her exactly the way I want.

The mask... she lifts it, just enough to expose my lips, her fingers trembling as they peel it off my face. Her lips crash down on mine with a carnal need, and for a moment, I can't tell where her breath ends and mine begins. She moves against me with ferocity, our bodies locked in an almost primal rhythm. My hands grip her hips tighter, pulling her down harder, guiding her movements as we both chase the edge of release.

Her body presses closer, her huge tits pressed firmly up against my chest as if she can't get enough, as if my sweet doe wants to drown in me.

Fuck, I am utterly consumed by her heat, the slick glide of her skin against mine, the way her breath hitches with every inch of me she takes.

I guide her harder, deeper, feeling the pulse of her movements, the way she shudders against me, her breath now mingling with mine as we get lost in the rhythm of each other's desire. She's so fucking tight, so *perfect*, I can barely think, barely breathe, just driven by instinct. The heady rush of pleasure builds with each grind, each pull of her body against mine.

Her hands claw at my vest as she throws herself forward, her lips brushing over my jaw, my neck. She's wild, hungry, desperate, and it drives me crazy. Her body trembles, and I feel every inch of her as she gets closer, her moans rising in pitch.

"Come on, baby," I growl against her lips, my voice hoarse, desperate. "Fucking give it to me. Let. Go."

With a final thrust, she does. Her back arches, her mouth falling open as she finally comes undone, her body shaking with the force of her release. The tightness around me pushes me over the edge. My balls tighten with impending release, and I can't hold back any longer. I bury myself deep within her, a final, guttural groan escaping my lips as I let go, filling her with every fucking drop I have to give.

"Fuck," I groan, gripping her hips tightly as I hold her down against me, forcing her to take every inch, every bit of me.

As we both come down from the high, our breaths still shallow and ragged, she suddenly pulls the mask entirely off.

Fuck.

For a second, everything stops. Time freezes.

Her eyes, half-lidded, flutter open, and when they meet mine—*realization* crashes into her. The joy, the ecstasy in her face falters, replaced by something else entirely— *horror.* She stiffens, her entire body going still, her gaze locked onto mine in disbelief. The breath hitches in her chest, and she pulls away, slowly, like she's seen a ghost, but it's not the one she's been fantasizing about.

I let her climb all the way off of me before I stand, my body cold despite the heat of our exchange, the intimacy shattering in an instant. A dark laugh bubbles up from deep in my chest as I tuck myself away.

"Crazy how much we look alike, isn't it?" I ask, my voice dark with satisfaction, dripping with something far less innocent than she ever imagined.

Her wide, panicked eyes lock onto mine, and for a moment, I savor the fear. The shock. I know what she's thinking—*This isn't him. This isn't Alex.*

She's breathing fast now, her gaze darting around, as if looking for an escape, some way to make sense of the moment. But there's no running from this. She doesn't understand how she ended up here, with me. She doesn't know how long I've been planning this, how carefully I've been setting this game in motion.

The realization hits her like a freight train. The part of her that was wondering how Alex changed so suddenly, how everything felt so *different*—she was so caught up in the moment, so deep in the thrill of the chase, she didn't care.

Her eyes flicker between confusion and disbelief, the pieces slowly coming together. But it's too late. There's no going back.

"Who are you?" she asks in a panic.

"You were never meant to be his, my *sweet* doe." My voice is soft, and the words come out like a caress. "You were always meant to be *mine*."

To be continued...

ABOUT THE AUTHORS

MELISSA MCSHERRY

Melissa is a Canadian stay-at-home mom to seven minions and is happily married to a very patient man. When she isn't writing or reading, she is chasing kids, cleaning, or downing her fifth coffee of the day while binge-watching TV or reading. As a writer of dark romance, usually dark fantasy romance, her books always include possessive men, and lots of bloodshed with the added touch of "WTF" moments and spice!

Connect with Melissa on Instagram or TikTok as @pagemastermama

READER FACEBOOK GROUP: **DARK & DEPRAVED READERS**

DANA LEEANN

Dana LeeAnn is an author of many genres, which include dark romance, contemporary romance, horror erotica, and romantic fantasy. She lives in northern Colorado with her two kids and husband. In her free time, Dana spends time enjoying the outdoors or finding a new project to dive head first into.

Connect with Dana on Instagram or TikTok as @danaleeannhunt

READER FACEBOOK GROUP: **DARK & DANGEROUS ROMANCE: DANA LEEANN READER GROUP**

Made in United States
Orlando, FL
02 December 2024